QUAKE

LISA
ARRINGTON

QUAKE

This book is a work of fiction. Names, characters, places and incidents either are products of the author's imagination or are used fictitiously. No part of this book can be reproduced in any form or by electronic or mechanical means including information storage and retrieval systems without the express written permission

CONTENTS

This book is dedicated to the two greatest
accomplishments of my life,

Qevon and Bryson.

I love you.

PROLOGUE

Sitting in the command center, she gazed over her unit, silently relishing in what was about to happen. "Have you secured her?" she asked, turning to face him.

"Yes, mistress, she has been secured."

A cold smile crept across her face. "You must keep her close; she and the others cannot escape."

He nodded, accepting the truth behind the words that his leader spoke.

She returned her attention to the monitors before them, watching as the other units prepared to descend around the world. "We will be moving up the time table to this week," she informed him.

"This week? Why?" He realized his response was unwelcomed and looked upon as a challenge to her authority.

"My apologies, mistress. I'm just surprised by the decision, it was my understanding that we wouldn't move for another month's time."

She looked down at him, the man she had chosen to be her second in command. The one that she had personally trained to be her commanding officer. She had made sure that he would be ready for the task when the time was right.

"Are you not able to complete your mission?" The look in her eye told him that there was only one answer. He stood, pinned underneath her gaze, sweat began to gather on his brow and he wondered if she could read the truth in his eyes. Standing at full attention, he lifted his chin and cleared his throat.

"Yes, mistress, I am. I just want to make sure that the other units are ready as well."

As she inspected him, she didn't sense any hesitation within him or his ability to move forward with the mission at hand.

"They will be," she assured him, once again turning to the screens, "they have to."

CHAPTER ONE

Ridgeway High School was all abuzz about the final basketball game happening that night. Ali sat with her best friend, Christine Lopez, under the cluster of trees with members of the varsity basketball team and cheerleaders. It was a crisp winter day for Tucson, but the temperature was holding steady at sixty-four degrees and they were going to make the most of it.

"Are you sure you don't want to eat in the cafeteria today?" Ali asked Christine for the second time. She plunked her tray down on the table and glanced around, looking for her boyfriend, DJ. They hadn't really talked since the party last weekend and she wasn't sure if she wanted to see him now or not.

"What is going on with you?" Christine asked as she sandwiched herself between her boyfriend, Zach, and Ali. "You've been acting mopey all week."

Ali poked at her Frito pie and shrugged. "Guess I'm coming down with something."

Best friends since seventh grade; Christine had always been able to tell when Ali was lying. The first day they met, Christine had found Ali crying in the girls' locker room. Ali had been upset because one of the popular girls had made fun of her, calling her flat chested and ugly.

When a feisty Hispanic girl, with warm brown eyes and curly black hair had asked her what was wrong, she lied and said she had hurt herself during the soccer game they had finished.

Christine took her in with those sharp eyes of hers and told her that if she wanted to sit there and lie that was fine, but if someone cared enough to stop and ask what was wrong, the least she could do was tell the truth. The brutal honesty of that logic startled Ali into telling her the truth.

The next day, during gym, Christine walked up to that girl and slapped her across the face, asking what gave her the right to go around judging others. From a part of the town called "Latin Squares" Christine had learned to take care of herself at a young age. She was outspoken, fearless and confident; no one ever messed with her or the ones she cared about.

She received detention for a week for doing that. Ali felt so guilty; she went to their gym teacher and explained what had happened.

Christine still had to complete her detention, but

afterwards her and Ali where inseparable.

Ali Morgan was the youngest of the group, having just turned seventeen a couple of weeks ago. She grew up on the west side of the town with her mother and her brother, Caden.

They were what you would call "Irish Twins" with only three hundred and sixty-four days separating them. Much to her brother's irritation, she had been able to skip the third grade, and join him in his fourth grade class.

They looked so much alike with their caramel complexions and grey-blue eyes that they had enjoyed being able to trick people into thinking that they were actual twins.

She looked at the tables around them and saw Caden standing with a group of cheerleaders, his arm around the shoulders of one of them. *Hmmm, that's new,* Ali mused to herself. She sensed DJ before she heard him come up and shake hands with Zach and exchange greetings with other members of the team; she both hated and loved how her body reacted to him. Before Christine could ask any more questions, she stood and plastered on a smile.

DJ took a quick look at her face and pulled her into a

hug. They held each other for a few seconds and she even gave his cheek a quick peck. *Huh, seems I'm not the only one uncomfortable.*

"So, you guys seem excited about the game tonight?" she heard Christine ask as she returned to her seat, with DJ taking the one across from her.

"Hell yeah," one of the players named Hardy called out.

"Brook Park isn't going to know what hit them!" Zach chimed in.

For the rest of the lunch hour, Ali and Christine mainly listened to the guys talk about strategy and about how awesome they are, throwing in an eye roll every now and then.

"Seven o'clock is not going to get here fast enough," Ali groaned when the bell rang, signaling the end of lunch.

Christine and Ali said good-bye to the guys and linked arms to head off to English class. Laughing and giggling, each took a turn mocking the basketball team. Ali felt better than she had all week.

❦

The gymnasium at Ridgeway High School was going

6

wild. Ali and Chris sat next to each other, cheering the guys on. Brook Park was up by two points and there was less than a minute left on the clock. DJ was making a fast break down the lane; Caden was on the three point line.

DJ faked left followed by a behind the back pass to Zach at his right who passed it to Caden, with just seconds left on the clock. Ali saw her brother catch the ball and send it skyward in one fluid motion. The crowd collectively held their breath as they watched it arc into the sky and start its slow decent.

"It's good!" the announcer called into the microphone and the crowd went wild. Students and parents alike flooded onto the court to celebrate with the team.

Coach Dunn thumped Zach, Caden and DJ on the back before heading to the announcer's table with Mr. Urrea, the school principal.

"Attention! Attention!" Mr. Urrea spoke into the microphone, trying to be heard above the din. "Ladies and gentlemen, attention, please!" The noise slowly began to die down, but the excitement was still in the air.

"What a game, what a game!" The mild-mannered principal wiped his brow with his handkerchief, smiling from ear to ear. "It is now time to award this season's first and second place trophies."

The principal walked over to the announcer's table and hefted up the smaller of the two huge trophies. "In second place; with an impressive season record of 25 and 2, the Brook Park Lions!"

There were a few cheers from the visitor's side and overall polite applause from the crowd as the team captain and co-captain walked to the center of the court to accept it on behalf of their team.

"And now, with great pleasure, I present this year's first place champions," again the crowd exploded in cheers, yells and whistles, "your Ridgeway Park Pumas!" Zach and DJ walked up to Mr. Urrea, each taking one side of the trophy and hoisting it in the air.

Zach threw a mischievous grin at Christine in the stands and took the microphone from Mr. Urrea. "Hey!" Zach spoke into the microphone, and unbelievably the crowd got even louder. "Hey, quiet down, bit--," Zach was cut off when Mr. Urrea placed a hand on his shoulder. The crowd laughed and settled down.

"Hey," Zach started again, throwing out a smile. The

captain of the basketball team, Zach Atwood, was the typical boy next door with blond hair and blue eyes and being an all-around good guy. He had every girl at Ridgeway High vying for his attention, but his heart belonged to only one and he looked directly at her as he spoke.

"As captain of this year's Puma basketball team and also on the behalf of the senior class, we want to thank Coach Dunn for his support and encouragement this season."

Zach then threw a quick look at the principal, and before he could stop him, he yelled, "We rocked this bitch!" The crowd erupted in cheers and cats calls. Mr. Urrea gave Zach a sharp look, then winked at him and shooed him towards the awaiting fans.

"Did you see that hero shot, sis?" Caden came bounding up to her, pulling her into a sweaty bear hug.

Ali laughed and playfully pushed him away. "Yeah, big brother, I did!" He released his grip on her when he saw DJ coming their way. They embraced each other. Everyone else groaned as Christine and Zach began a very public display of affection.

"Hey, y'all think you two can wrap this up?" Caden asked, "I'm starving!" After a few more minutes, and the team threatening to douse them with the water cooler, they finally came up for air.

Christine and Ali moved to the side of the court and watched as the team posed for pictures for faculty, press and parents alike. Once that was over the guys retreated to the locker room for one final talk with the coach and to get changed. The girls gathered their things and walked into the chilly night air towards the parking lot.

※

"Too bad your mom couldn't make it tonight." Christine zipped up her jacket. Ali hadn't noticed how warm it had been in the gym until they had gotten outside and the cold air touched bare skin.

"Yeah, but you know Caden, he'll tell her all about it tonight." She nudged Christine with her elbow. "I can't believe you two."

"I have no idea what you are talking about." Christine batted her eyelashes innocently and the girls dissolved into a fit of giggles.

"You two keep it up like that and DJ is likely to start

getting more ideas," Ali cautioned light-heartedly as they approached the car that she shared with Caden.

Christine came to a halt, throwing Ali a bit off balance.

"You mean, you two…" Christine trailed off, unable to hide her surprise.

Ali instantly regretted bringing this up. "No, we haven't," she said quickly, looking back towards the gym, wishing the guys would hurry up.

"Wow," Christine said quietly. "You mean that…since you two have been together…what? Almost a year now? And not once?"

Ali could feel her cheeks heat up and knew where this was going to lead. "Chris, not tonight, okay?" Ali asked her, looking down at her shoe, tapping it against the tire.

"Yeah, okay."

Once Ali looked up, her friend added, "I'm sure DJ hears that a lot." Christine laughed loudly, but when she saw the tears forming in Ali's eyes she stopped cold. "Wait. At the party." Ali could see the pieces falling into place in her friend's head. "That's what's been wrong with you all week!" Christine pulled Ali into a hug. "Is it really that bad, honey?"

Ali hugged her back. "He threatened to break up with me," she admitted, "talking something about how we don't have much time."

"That bastard! I can't believe he would do that." Christine started muttering something in Spanish under her breath. She was just about to say something when they both heard, "Oh! Girl on girl action! Can I get in on this?"

When they looked up they saw that the guys had wrapped things up and they were all walking towards the parking lot. "Later," Christine whispered and gave her a quick squeeze, and then louder, "You are such a pig, Hardy!" She was responded to with a chorus of pig sounds from the guys that continued as they caught up with them.

DJ came up to Ali and grabbed her hand, giving her another questioning look that Christine now understood.

"So, are we going to Freddy's or what?" Caden asked the group, "I need food!"

"You always need food," Ali responded, rolling her eyes.

"Well, I'm a growing boy." Caden smiled. The guys

groaned at the awful innuendo.

"Let's just get going," Zach suggested.

Ali walked to the driver's side of their car and unlocked it. "You aren't going to ride with me, babe?" DJ had a hint of sadness in his voice.

"Well, um." Ali glanced over at Caden for help, but as usual, her brother was oblivious to what was going on; snuggling up to his girl by the trunk.

"Ali," Christine called out, "you said you needed to talk to me about the test in fourth period, remember?" Zach gave Christine a questioning look, as he had the same class with Ali and knew that there was no test.

"Oh, that's right!" Ali walked back to DJ and gave him a quick kiss on the cheek. "I'll see you at Freddy's in a minute." Then she turned on her heel, threw the keys to Caden and ran to Zach's truck.

"Okay, what's up with you, Ali?" Zach asked as he backed his truck out of the lot.

"Nothing," she muttered as she looked out the window and watched as DJ walked dejectedly to his car.

"Nothing my ass," Zach snorted, "come on, Ali, spill

it."

Ali sighed and gave in when she saw Christine give her an encouraging nod. "Me and DJ got into a fight on Saturday. It's cool now," she lied.

"Yeah, so cool, that you are sitting here, in my truck, next to my girlfriend and making me miss out on some serious red light action," Zach teased. Christine lightly punched him on the thigh and then put a protective arm around Ali.

"Any guy that gives you a 'sleep with me or else' ultimatum doesn't deserve a girl like you," Christine stated matter of fact.

"He did what?" Zach growled.

"It doesn't matter. We're working it out. It's just…" Ali trailed off, looking at the huge sign that read Freddy's Hamburgers. Zach expertly pulled into a parallel spot and put the truck in park.

"Listen, I try to stay out of your business as much as this one lets me," he said, hooking a thumb towards Christine. "But seriously, if you need me to talk to him and tell him to back off, let me know." He glanced over Christine's head to make sure Ali was listening.

"Seriously, 'cause you know what will happen if Caden finds out."

Ali sighed and nodded her head. She did not want her brother hearing about this. She was embarrassed enough.

They all piled out of the truck and went to the front to wait for everyone to arrive. It only took a few minutes for the team to gather up and grab their favorite tables near the jukebox. Ali sat next to DJ and leaned into him as he put his arm around her shoulder.

"Look, I'm sorry," he whispered. "I shouldn't have said that the other night."

Ali turned her head slightly "Let's talk later," she whispered into his ear. He gave her a small smile and nod, relief washing over his face.

DJ Wilson came from the 'right side' of tracks. His family owned several successful businesses throughout Tucson and Arizona as a whole.

He never had to wait for the newest shoes to go on sale or worry about getting stuck with a clunker. He was the envy of most of the guys on the team due to his Nike collection alone, but he was still a pretty down-to-earth guy, that made good choices and was respectful, most of the time.

He knew that he had overstepped a line with Ali the other night and he would do anything for a chance to take it back. He wanted to blame his raging hormones for his behavior, but he couldn't. School was almost over and he knew they didn't have much time together left. He needed Ali to know how much he loved her, but forcing her into something was not the way to do it. He understood that now.

Once everyone had had their fill and the last quarter had been placed in the jukebox, it was time to continue the victory celebration by heading to Starr Pass, a dead-end spot out in the Tucson desert with a fire pit, an unobstructed view of the stars and a few hidden spots for getting up to no good.

Zach and Christine, Ali and DJ, Caden and his new girlfriend, Gemma, and a couple of her friends walked towards the pit while gathering old mesquite wood to light a fire. Ali shook her head as they walked off, every time they came out, they always vowed to gather enough wood for a few visits or even buy a cord from the nearby gas station, but somehow they always forgot.

"Are you really, okay?" Christine asked Ali, leading her

away from the group.

"Yeah, I'm okay." She gave her friend a reassuring smile. "It just made me think, ya know?"

"Think about what?" Gemma asked, bounding up, still dressed in her cheerleading uniform. Gemma Curtis had just moved to town six months ago. She had clear blue eyes that seemed to have a silvery glow, short blond hair and an ever-present perkiness that got a bit annoying at times.

She and Ali had never spent any real quality time together, so she wasn't sure if she could trust her not to run to Caden with what was going on; as always Christine took care of the situation.

"Nothing, nosey," Christine snapped.

"Oh, well isn't little Miss Bitchy coming out early tonight?" Gemma sneered back.

"Puta, you haven't seen anything yet, keep it up."

Gemma's eyes were as cold as ice as she pulled her hair behind her. She looked as if she was about to say something else to Christine, but turned around and went to talk with her friend, Michelle, another cheerleader that had come to the pass with her boyfriend, Bobby, a second string player on the team.

"What is up with you two?" Ali asked while watching Gemma sit with her back to them, leaning in close to speak with Michelle. Ali never understood Christine's instant dislike with Gemma.

"I don't know there's just something about her," Christine said, as she pulled her hair back into a ponytail. Gemma's head turned towards them for a second before twisting back around when one of the guys laughed out loud in the distance. "I don't trust her."

꙳

The fire was bright and set the mood for the rest of the evening. Ali, DJ, Zach and Christine sat in front of the pit talking about their week at school and rehashing the vital points of the basketball game, including Caden's buzzer beater.

Gemma, Michelle and Bobby kept to themselves, heads bent together closely, leaving Caden to act as the bridge between to the two groups. A little after ten o'clock, couples started to wander off, either back to their cars or other private spots just off the path.

Ali was snuggled in DJ's arms, drifting off to sleep when he nudged her awake. "Hey, sleepy head, we need to talk," he whispered into her ear.

"Now? Can't it wait?" Her head was foggy with sleep and she couldn't remember why they needed to talk.

"Yes, now." He stood up and held his hand out for her to take. "It really can't wait."

Ali looked up into his face and the memory came rushing back. She took a deep breath and took his hand. DJ led her to his car, parked at the edge of the parking lot. He started the car and turned on the heater to keep the chill at bay.

"So, what's up?" Ali licked her lips and played with the tips of her braids, not meeting DJ's eyes.

DJ gently cupped her chin and pulled her to meet his. "About Saturday night," he began.

"DJ, wait." She placed a hand on his arm. "I've been thinking about what you said all week, and…"

DJ held a finger up to her lips. "I am willing to wait," DJ told her. "For as long as you need me to. I will never try to push you into anything or try to rush you again."

Tears began to fill her eyes as she looked into his. "Do you mean it?" Ali whispered.

DJ answered by pulling her in for a soft kiss. "I was being a jerk and insensitive. I know it isn't a good excuse, but it is what it is." The look on his face begged for her to understand. "I am so sorry, Ali."

She leaned across the console and kissed him on his cheek. "I'm sorry too." She tried to cross her legs in the small space and failed. "I reacted badly and I shouldn't have stormed out like that." She tilted her head against the seat and glanced out the window. "I just... I've never..." Ali whispered, her breath fogging up the window.

"I know. You've never made love before."

Ali nodded her head, unsure of why this was embarrassing her.

"To tell the truth... neither have I. I just need you to know how much I love you. Before... it just wasn't the right time or the right place." DJ cringed at the memory. "And it sure as hell wasn't the right guy, the way I was trying to push you into doing something you weren't ready for. It's just... I feel that we don't have much time left," he trailed off. "You know, with school ending in a few months and us having to decide what to do afterwards."

Ali turned and faced DJ, shocked by his admission. "When you do decide that you're ready to go that far," he took a deep breath, "and if it's with me, I'll be waiting."

Ali hadn't realized that she had started crying until she felt DJ wipe a tear away from her cheek. He got out of the car and walked around to her side to open her car door. Holding out his hand to assist her, he pulled her into him, cupping her face and pulling her in for a not-so-gentle kiss before returning to the fire pit.

It was approaching midnight and it was time for everyone to pack up and go home. Ali and Christine cuddled together under a blanket Zach had stashed behind the seat of his truck, while the guys stomped out the fire.

Even though the basketball season was officially over, the team still had to meet early tomorrow morning for a press conference and talk with scouts from various colleges that had come out to see them play.

Ali knew that Zach, DJ and Caden approached and they would have to make some tough decisions. She felt a slight twinge of guilt go through her when she thought about her own future and all of the college acceptance letters she had hidden under her mattress.

"What are you going to do if Zach signs with UCLA?" Ali asked Christine to lighten her mood.

"Follow him anywhere," Christine replied dreamily.

Ali giggled. She could totally see Christine packing up and moving to California without a single look back.

"Wouldn't it be great if they all got signed together?" Christine asked as she yawned. "Then we could find somewhere big enough for all of us!"

"Yeah, wouldn't that be so grand?" they heard Gemma's voice, heavy with sarcasm, behind them. "Well, not to bust anyone's bubble, but that just isn't going to happen." She skipped up to Caden before either girl could reply; leaving them wondering what her words meant.

"Don't pay her any attention," Zach said, coming up and scooping Christine into his arms.

"Did you get any letters yet, Ali?" DJ asked, putting an arm around her shoulders.

"Nope, not yet." she said a little too forcefully. "How

about you guys? Have you already decided who you're going to commit to?"

DJ shrugged his shoulders. "I'm hoping we can go to the same school… even if it is University of Arizona."

Ali shuddered suddenly. She had every intention of getting out of Tucson, out of Arizona period if she could help it.

"Are you cold, babe?" DJ took off his jacket and put it over hers. She was cold, but the temperature had nothing to do with it.

CHAPTER TWO

Lying in bed, gray clouds hanging low in the sky with a chill in the air, Ali couldn't picture a more perfect Saturday morning.

Tucson was famous for the heat and its sunny skies three-hundred and fifty-five days of the year, but it was the other eleven that Ali always craved.

Hearing sounds of life in the kitchen; she rolled out of bed and grabbed the pajama bottoms that she had kicked herself out of in her sleep.

"Morning, Mom," she yawned out, walking to the cabinet to grab a box of cereal.

"Morning, sweetheart." Lanie Morgan pressed a quick kiss on top of her daughter's head.

"C already out?" Ali took the bowl and cup of coffee from her mother.

"Yeah, he left about a half hour ago."

"Hmmm," Ali replied, while adding cream to her coffee, then sighing as the first sip slid down her throat. She heard her mom chuckle but then she did the same thing herself.

Lanie Morgan wasn't your typical mom. She had had a semi-charmed life growing up, somewhat popular, smart as a whip and very pretty. Ali tilted her head to the side and looked at her mom standing by the window, coffee in one hand, tablet in the other.

She thought she favored her. They were both slight in frame, had a warm caramel complexion and shared the strange blue-grey eyes that had most people asking if they wore contacts.

She had always wondered if Caden looked like their father. Ali had heard the story of how their parents had met a thousand times. When Lanie had graduated from Ridgeway High, Grandpa and Grandma Morgan had taken her on a trip as a gift. They had gone to Bermuda to visit family, then Ohio for her father's union and finally to California for some beach time before returning home.

While in Ohio, one of Grandpa's best friends suggested that it would be nice for his nephew to take Lanie out one afternoon and get her out of the house and away from "all the old folks." When she spoke to the young man on the phone, she was so happy to be getting away from her parents, she hadn't really thought any more about it.

When Darrell Anthony appeared to pick her up, he was

'a cup of coffee with just the right amount of cream,' Lanie had mused during one recount. A few months later he proposed and an eighteen-year-old Lanie left home to be with him, much to her parent's dismay. Grandma once told her that they had even tried to bribe her to come back, but it didn't work.

A marriage never did happen, and two years later she returned, with two babies on her hips. But that hadn't slowed her down. Now with two mouths to feed and on her own, she put herself through night school; studying computer science, while working full time during the day. She had graduated with top honors with her two biggest fans in the crowd, cheering her on.

Ali remembered asking about her father when she was younger, and instead of bashing her ex-boyfriend as some women would have, she simply stated that 'some people just aren't cut out to be parents.' Back then, Ali didn't understand what that had meant, but she understood now, and was thankful every day that her mom was such a person.

They sat in companionable silence a few minutes longer, when Ali saw her mom smirk over something on the tablet.

"How long are you going to sit there and stare at me?" She chuckled as she set her cup down and sat next to her daughter.

"You caught me, huh?"

Lanie playfully pulled Ali's braids. "Looks like it's time to redo your braids. Do you want me to make the appointment or will you do it?"

Ali ran her hand over her scalp and sure enough, the new growth was about an inch out. "I'll call later today," she promised.

"So what's going on in that pretty brain of yours?" Lanie stood up and reached for the coffee pot to refill both their cups. Ali chewed on her bottom lip, debating if she should confide in her mom about the letters she had been receiving and the plans she was making.

The phone rang giving her a temporary reprieve. "Hello, Morgan residence," Lanie said in a clear, bright voice. "It's for you. It's Chris."

Ali took the phone from her mom and walked out of the kitchen. "What's up, girl?" Ali plunked down on the sofa and turned on the TV.

"Hey chica, would you and Caden be down for some camping this weekend?" Ali could hear Christine's little brother crying in the background.

"What's wrong with Nando?" Ali asked, flipping to the weather channel.

"Girl, I don't know, my mom told him he couldn't have something and now he's all butt hurt about it." Suddenly there was a crash, silence then more crying. "Oh shit." Christine told her to think about it and call her back, then hung up in rush.

"What did Christine want?" Lanie asked, walking to the sofa.

"She wanted to know if Caden and I wanted to go camping this weekend." She was looking intently at the weather channel and while the temperature was going to be a bit chilly for camping, it wouldn't be totally unbearable.

"And whose parents are going to be with you?"

Ali gave her a blank look.

"Um, we didn't get that far into the conversation." Ali knew that this was a parentis non gratis trip, and would bet money that her mom knew it as well. Lanie shook her head laughing and disappeared from the room. When she returned holding a small package, Ali groaned.

While most kids would cringe if their parent ever brought up the sex talk, Ali and Caden had their mom's spiel memorized. Lanie had always been very candid and open, preparing her children for the 'one thing led to another' situations.

"Mom, I have no intentions of losing my virginity to DJ during this trip or anytime in the near future. I don't even know if we're going camping or not yet!" Just then she heard Caden come barreling in through the backdoor.

"Caden, we're in here!" Ali called out to her brother, hoping that he would become their mother's new target. "How did your meetings go?" She sat up and scooted over so he could sit next to her.

"Really good, sis!" He gave his mom a quick kiss on the cheek and went to sit down. "I met with coaches from the U of A, ASU and UCLA." He went into details about each coach and what happened during each meeting, bouncing in his seat with excitement. "Zach and DJ spoke with the UCLA coach as well, which was really cool!"

Lanie beamed with pride, as her oldest continued to weigh the pros and cons of each college that wanted him to play for them. And while Ali's plan to detract the attention from her had succeeded, she couldn't help but feel a little resentment towards Caden being able to go anywhere he wanted without a second's hesitation from their mother.

Once Caden had given his full report, Ali brought up the camping trip and he wholeheartedly agreed.

"Great, I'll go call Christine." She grabbed the house phone and ducked into the kitchen, hiding a smile when their mom launched into Caden with her 'you never know' speech.

❦

It had been settled, Zach would borrow his dad's Explorer so he could pick up Christine, Ali and DJ. Caden would use their car to go get Gemma, when Ali heard that Gemma was coming along, she silently groaned. Christine would love that piece of news. Ali borrowed one of Caden's duffel bags and packed her warmest clothes, borrowing a knit hat and scarf from her mom's closet.

"Have everything you need?" Lanie asked, while leaning

on the doorframe.

Ali sighed, reiterating that she was not going to sleep with DJ, when Lanie held up her hand to cut her off.

"Who knows, it may not happen, or it may. I just want you two to be careful. I don't want anything happening that will make you give up or have to put your future on hold." Opening her mouth to protest one final time, Lanie threw the small box to her daughter.

"Just pack the damn things."

The radio was blasting, Ali and Christine were singing along in the backseat while Zach drove and DJ navigated up Mt. Lemmon. It was the only spot in Tucson that was guaranteed to also be at least twenty degrees cooler than the valley during the summer months.

With its lush pine trees, beautiful maples and tall oaks, it was easy to forget that just a few miles south of here was rock, tumbleweeds and cactus. Zach pulled into Rose Canyon Lake, one of their favorite camping spots. It was an absolutely gorgeous spot, a secluded lake surrounded by pines and oaks, which had begun to change color with the season.

Zach parked next to the trailhead. "Alright, ladies, while you pack up all the gear and set up the tents, we'll be here," he teased. Christine lightly punched him in the arm, grabbing her backpack and duffle bag.

DJ took Ali's duffle bag and his in one hand while carrying a tent in the other. She was about to protest, but grabbed one of the cords of wood instead, sticking her tongue out at him. Thankfully the site wasn't far from the trail and it only took a few trips to get everything out of the truck.

By the time Caden and Gemma arrived, all the tents had been set up and a fire was going full blaze. Since this was Gemma's first time camping, Zach was showing her how to use the food lockers, in case of bears that may come around the area. "But since it's so cool out now, we probably won't see one," he assured her when she began to freak out.

"Are you sure? I mean, what should we do if one does come out here?" She looked around the site, sure that a bear was lurking just behind the tree line.

"Don't run for starters." Zach chuckled. "But seriously, we'll go over it once you and Caden are all settled in." He gave her a warm smile and then went to help the guys finish up.

Christine rolled her eyes, but kept her mouth shut. She had promised Zach that she wouldn't be mean to Gemma this trip and would take a chance to get to know her before judging her too quickly.

She invited Gemma to join her and Ali around the campfire when the boys decided they wanted to go fishing and catch something for dinner that night. Gemma hesitated, but nodded, accepting the invitation.

"I cannot believe my mom gave me condoms," Ali moaned to the girls. Christine began to laugh hysterically. "Chris! This is truly mortifying. What if I come home with them? Or worse, what if I don't?" Ali's face slumped as she wondered which would be the worst case scenario.

"I don't see what's so bad about that," Gemma spoke up, her clear blue eyes sparkling. "I mean, she's just looking out for you guys… you know?" She tucked her hair behind her ear, afraid she may be speaking out of turn. Ali was beginning to realize that it was a nervous habit of hers.

"She's right, Ali," Christine said. "I mean, my own parents pretty much abandoned me and expected me to be an unwed mother before I turned sixteen."

Ali knew that Christine was just as grateful for her mom as she was. "She just doesn't want you to go through what she did."

Ali let out a sigh. "I know, guys, but we just had the talk about waiting." She threw her hands out in frustration. "What is he going to think?"

"Don't tell him?" Gemma asked.

"Hide them in one of our bags?" Christine offered.

"No, I should keep them with me." She shook her head at the next words that came out of her mouth.

"Just in case."

🙡

Dusk fell early, but the fire was roaring and there were plates of hot, delicious fish being passed around and plenty of blankets to snuggle into. Zach, Caden, and DJ had managed to catch enough bluegill to feed everyone at dinner.

Ali had laughed at Christine and Gemma's faces as they tried to help clean the fish. She thought that they were going to pass out when it came time to gut them. By the end, it seemed as if that little experience had created a new bond between them and she could see that they were both more relaxed around each other.

After dinner, they all snuggled into blankets and made hot chocolate and s'mores. Ali didn't know if it was being out of town, or if it was the scenery or the hot chocolate; but the sense of camaraderie was definitely in the air. Ali and DJ snuggled deeper into the blanket, while holding on to the mugs that warmed them.

Caden and Zach where pouring sand into the last embers of the grill, while Christine coached Gemma on how to add more wood to the fire.

"Having fun?" Ali asked Gemma, whose flushed cheeks gave her a rosy glow.

"I'm having a blast!" she confided. "I never thought camping could be this fun, we never did anything like this back home." Her face fell at those last words.

"Hey, are you okay?" Christine asked, gently placing a hand on her shoulder.

"Um… yeah," she said, quickly turning away and walking towards Caden.

"What was that all about?" Christine asked.

"I have no idea."

As expected later in the evening, the discussion turned to the press conference and the meetings with the scouts. Zach and DJ were pretty sure they were going to commit to the U of A, while Caden was considering UCLA.

"Come on guys!" Caden stood up, swiping dust off his backside. "California, beaches, ba--" he cut himself off, glancing over at Gemma with a sly grin. "We would be out on our own," he rationalized.

"We can be out on our own here in our hometown," Zach threw back at him.

Ali sat back, not speaking a word. She knew this was the time to bring up the acceptance letters from the schools on the east coast, but she was afraid of her friend's reactions.

"Yeah, but Tucson doesn't have Disneyland!" Caden threw back, as if that alone should cinch the deal.

"Well, I applied to all the schools that Zach applied to and got accepted to U of A." Christine beamed proudly.

"Ah, so that's it," Caden mused.

"Ali, where have you applied?" Christine asked her.

There was a curious look on her face, definitely brought on by her lack of participation. "Um, a few places," she answered, licking her lips. It was now or never. She sat up straighter and squared her shoulders. "I've applied to and been accepted to UConn, Spelman and Cornell." She took a deep breath and went for it, "I accepted Spelman's offer of a full four-year scholarship."

Ali began to count the seconds of silence in her head.

One one-thousand

Two one-thousand

Three one-thousand

Four one-thousand

Five one-thousand

"You did what?" Caden whispered.

She took a deep breath and repeated her answer, "I accepted Spelman's offer of a full four-year scholarship." She looked around the campfire at her friends and brother. "They have an excellent Political Sciences program… and they're the only one that will give me a scholarship. I would be crazy to turn this down!"

Ali's gaze rested on Caden's face. He looked at her like she had grown two heads.

"I can't believe this," he said as he stood once again, his blue-grey eyes ablaze. "This is a joke right? You seriously can't be considering leaving!"

Ali buckled under her brother's stare, and was surprised by the strength in her own voice. "It's not a joke. I start this fall."

"Ali, are you really going to Atlanta?" Christine asked.

"No, she's not," Caden answered for her. "You can't leave Mom here by herself!" Caden began pacing back and forth. "Mom doesn't even know, does she?" Caden accused her.

"No, she doesn't know. And yes, I am leaving." Ali stood up and looked her brother dead in the eye. "You aren't the only one that has dreams of being on your own. Did it ever cross your mind that I might want to get out of here as much as you do?"

Hot tears began to fill her eyes. "I have a great idea,

Caden, if you don't want Mom to be alone, then *you* stay here." She turned and stalked off to the tent.

She could hear the others talking about her in raised voices, but she didn't care. How dare Caden tell her what she could and could not do! She was so angry, she slapped the ground as hard as she could and was surprised when it shook. Ali could hear cries from the others outside and tried to make her way to the tent flap.

"Did you guys feel that?" she called out, as she tried to get out of the tent, only to lose her balance as the ground shook with more intensely.

CHAPTER THREE

Ali heard cries coming from all directions as she tried to regain her balance with the earth shaking beneath her feet.

"What the hell?" she heard Zach cry out.

Finally, able to keep her balance she made her way out of the tent, what she saw reminded her of a shaking a snow globe. The shaking slowly stopped and everyone stared at each other for a few seconds.

"Is everyone okay?" DJ asked the group, getting a chorus of nodding heads and shaky yeah's.

"Was that an earthquake?" Christine asked in disbelief.

"That was an earthquake," Caden replied, pulling Gemma into him.

"No way, here?" Zach obviously knew that it was possible, but just couldn't believe it.

They all started talking at once and checking over the campsite.

"Wait!" Ali cried out. "Wait, what about the cars?" It suddenly dawned on everyone that if their modes of transportation were disabled, they would be in serious trouble. Zach and DJ ran down the trail and they heard a curse.

"The truck's okay," they yelled back, "but your guy's car is scrap."

Caden started down the path, but the guys where already headed back up. "A tree fell. It missed the truck by inches; your car got the impact."

Caden and Ali ran down the path to see for themselves. And sure enough, their car looked like a pancake. Dejected, they walked back to the campsite.

"Do you think that it hit the valley?" Christine asked, suddenly worried about their families.

Ali and Caden just shrugged, not sure of the answer.

"Oh man, my mom is going to freak if I don't call soon," Gemma whined.

"The cells don't get reception up here, but we could go down to the payphones," Caden offered as he put his arm around her shoulders.

"That's a good idea," Ali agreed.

Ali and DJ went to look for the flashlights while the others sat around the campfire.

"I'm sorry," she whispered to DJ as they went through their packs. "I should have told you sooner."

DJ just shrugged, but remained quiet.

"DJ," Ali began.

"Look, Ali, we'll talk about it later, okay?"

The gruffness is in his voice made Ali realize that now wasn't a good time, so meekly she said, "Okay."

When they returned to the pit, DJ handed Caden one of the flashlights.

"I think it would be best if just the two of us went," Caden suggested. "It will be easier for me to guide just Gemma and myself."

He pointedly looked at his sister, who was beginning to understand that no one really wanted to be around her just then.

"Okay, we'll give you thirty minutes to get there and back," Zach announced, "if you're not back by then I'll try to maneuver the truck down the trail."

"Zach, no," Christine said. "You don't know what the roads are like and its pitch black out there. You wouldn't know you were in trouble until it was too late."

The guys nodded their heads in agreement and contemplated their situation.

"Look, me and Gemma should be able to get down to the payphones, call our parents and hopefully a ranger station, and be back within forty-five minutes. If we're not back by then, come looking for us by foot. That's going to be the safest way," Caden rationalized.

Everyone agreed to the new plan. Ali and Christine offered Gemma their scarfs and gloves since she hadn't brought any, and extra socks as the temperature was dropping fast.

"Okay." Caden looked around to make sure he had the flashlight and a hunting knife with him. "Let's get going."

Ali walked over to her brother and hugged him. "Be safe," she whispered into his ear and gave him a quick peck on the cheek.

He was ridged for a second, but returned the hug. "Always, Ali."

Zach checked his watch and set the timer as Caden and Gemma waved good-bye and disappeared into the darkness.

Ali and Christine sat by the fire with refilled mugs in their hands, watching DJ and Zach discuss their next move. It was decided that they would wait for Caden and Gemma to return, but they wouldn't drive down the mountain till daybreak.

"Awesome," Ali said. "Guess this means the camping trip is cut short." She was hoping for a couple of chuckles to lighten the mood, but no one responded to the bad joke.

"So, when were you going to tell me?" Christine confronted her instead.

Ali couldn't mistake the hurt she heard in her best friend's voice. "I don't know." Ali shrugged, throwing a blanket around her shoulder. She knew that she had to tell everyone at some point, but she had avoided it every time the conversation had come up.

"Why the east coast?"

"I just need to get out of here," Ali admitted. "I love my family and I love you guys." Her voice cracked and she took a deep breath to settle herself. "I need to find myself, Chris." She looked into her chocolate brown eyes and prayed that she would understand.

Christine sniffed and looked over her shoulder at the guys, still in intense debate over something. Slowly she turned her head back towards Ali and with a huge smile said, "You better write me, bitch."

Ali let out a squeal of delight and hugged her friend tightly. "Thank you so much for understanding." She felt tears prickle her eyes.

"I love you, Ali." Christine hugged her back. "And I know that you aren't doing this to hurt anyone, it's just." Christine pulled back, biting her lip.

"What, Chris?"

"It's just that, I admire you."

Ali sat there stunned. She had longed for Christine's strength since the day they met. "What are you talking about, girl?"

Christine turned around once more to make sure the guys were still deep in discussion. "I never would have been brave enough to do that," she admitted sheepishly.

Ali was about to tell her she was crazy and could do anything she set her mind to do, but they both heard a branch snap and turned to see that DJ and Zach approaching them.

"Later," Christine promised her with a squeeze of her hand.

⚘

They continued to sit around the fire in tense silence, constantly checking their watches and time as it slowly ticked by. Ali was pacing back and forth, ready to head down the trail to find her brother, when she heard footsteps crunching on the path.

DJ and Zach stood in front of Christine and Ali, fists clenched, ready to defend if necessary. Finally, a beam of light quickly appeared, followed by Caden and Gemma. Ali jumped up and ran to him, grasping him tightly.

"I am so glad you're back."

Caden returned the hug and then faced the group. "The payphones are out, and no phones at the ranger station either."

"Are you serious?" DJ threw his hands up in

frustration.

"As a heart attack."

"We would have been back sooner, but we weren't the only ones to think of using the phone," Gemma explained. "The Ranger told everyone to go back to their campsites and to wait until morning to try to get down. They are trying to see how damaged the roads are and don't want anybody trying to leave."

As if on cue, they heard several vehicles on the road.

"Idiots," Zach muttered under his breath. "Okay, well, I vote that we stay put until at least daybreak and then go from there."

Everyone nodded in agreement.

After that, the night was more subdued. Christine tried to get everyone to tell ghost stories. Ali suggested stargazing and Zach and DJ thought s'mores would lighten the mood, but nothing worked.

Around midnight, everyone gave up and decided it was time to call it a night.

"Night, guys," Ali called out as she slipped into the tent she was sharing with DJ. He followed her and zipped up the flap.

Ali sat on her sleeping bag, waiting, wondering if he would talk to her now or if he would remain quiet until morning. DJ took off his jacket and bunched it up to use as a pillow. He lay down on his sleeping bag, back turned to Ali. She let out a sigh and got into her bag. They laid there in silence for a few minutes.

"My mom gave me condoms."

As expected, he snorted. "Do you really think that sex is going to make up for not telling me?"

She rolled her eyes and prayed for strength. "No, but it did get you to talk to me."

DJ snorted again. "Okay, it did." He rolled himself over so that he could face her.

"Why did you hide that?" That was one of the things she loved about DJ, he never beat around the bush.

"I don't know." Ali shrugged. "I was afraid that if I told anyone, they would talk me out of it. They would say how I needed to stay here because Caden would be leaving."

"Yeah... what was up with that? Why do you have to stay if Caden leaves?"

He heard Ali take a deep breath before she replied, "It's because my mom treats us differently." She took another deep breath. "She's always been more protective with me than him. Curfews are different, unless I'm with him. He can slack off at home, but I'm expected to make sure everything is done. I get straight A's, while he doesn't, but I'm the only one lectured about how important school is." She stopped when she got close to the real issue.

"What babe?" She felt DJ's hand searching for hers. "What aren't you telling me?"

When she spoke, her voice was thick with emotion. "For as long as I can remember; she has always said the same thing."

"What?"

"That Caden was going to reach his dream of being a basketball star and I was going to be home with her, cheering him on."

*

"Are we there yet?" Caden moaned from the back row.

Christine threw her gum wrapper at him. "How old are you? Two?" She was in a foul mood due to lack of sleep.

They were slowly making their way down the mountain, with what seemed like hundreds of others who had also decided to wait until the safety of morning.

"This is going to take forever." Gemma sighed.

Ali sensed a nasty remark coming from Christine and decided to divert.

"So, Gemma, you're from Detroit, right?" Ali twisted around in the seat, effectively blocking her best friend's view.

"Um, yeah, I am," she said nervously.

"I've never been, but hear it's a great city," Ali offered. "The birth place of Motown, right?" she asked, hoping it would pull her into more conversation.

Gemma just shrugged and looked out the window.

"Did you spend a winter there?" DJ asked, picking up on Gemma's unusual reluctance to talk about her past.

"What is with you two?" Caden yawned out; not seeming to notice the dirty look Gemma threw at DJ. "Is this the Spanish Inquisition or something?" he teased. "Let the girl rest, she had a long night." He winked at her and she gave him a small smile while Ali and DJ groaned at the innuendo.

The group slowly inched their way forward, continuously trying their cells hoping for a signal the further down they went.

"Anyone got anything?" Zach asked, knowing the answer.

The choruses of 'no's' confirmed his thought.

They had been in the truck for over two hours now and getting a little stir crazy. Christine flipped through the CD's and available radio stations. Caden and DJ talked about their college options again.

Gemma gazed out the window. Ali made herself as small as possible, hoping that they wouldn't draw her into another confrontation about her own college plans.

After another hour, they finally approached the main entrance of the park and they couldn't believe their eyes. There, running parallel with the road was a large crack. Zach slowed when they were approached by a Park Ranger.

"Howdy" he said, "you young folks have any trouble last night?"

"Why yes, sir, we did. A tree landed on my friend's car."

The Ranger shook his head.

"What site were you at?"

Zach gave him the information and provided Caden and Ali's contact information.

"Alright, it should be safe travels from this point on, but take it slow," the Ranger warned.

"Well, thanks, sir. We'll take it slow." The Ranger tipped his hat as Zach rolled up the window and pulled forward.

A few minutes later, they had reached the base of the mountain and saw no further signs of the earthquake.

"Hey, isn't there a grocery store up ahead?" Caden whispered, not wanting to disturb Gemma, who had fallen asleep.

"Yeah, there is. Let's stop there. We should get cell coverage there for sure and if it doesn't work, they should have a phone to use," Zach told him.

When they arrived, Ali, DJ and Christine went into the

store to see if they could use the phone, while Caden walked to various spots of the lot searching for a signal. Much to their dismay, the store manager was standing at the door to inform them that the power was out and they wouldn't be allowed in the store.

"We just need to make a call!" Christine protested.

"I'm sorry, but it would be a liability if I allowed you to go around the store in the dark."

After a few more minutes pleading their case to deaf ears, they returned to the car and filled everyone in.

"And there's still no cell signal," Caden grunted, climbing back into the truck. "Let's just get to someone's house and go from there."

⁂

The truck came to a stop at Caden and Ali's, Lanie standing in the doorway ready to rush down the drive.

"Oh, thank goodness!" She embraced both her children and then gave the others a quick look over to make sure they were safe.

"Yes, Mom, we're fine," Caden assured her, hugging her back.

"Ms. Morgan, is your phone working?" Gemma asked in her voice small. "I would really like to call my parents and let them know I'm okay."

Lanie glanced at Gemma and told her where to find the phone.

Tears were streaming down Lanie's face. "I was about to go out there and try to find you guys." She pulled them in again and held them tight.

"Are you okay, Mom. Were you hurt?"

Lanie just snorted. "I lived in California and slept through a 7.5, that one had nothing on it." She gave them a smile and reached to dry the tears. "Are you guys hungry? Do you need some coffee?" She turned towards the house and immediately made herself busy in the kitchen.

Zach, Christine, DJ and Gemma took turns using the phone, leaving shortly thereafter. Ali and Caden filled their mom in on the camping trip, and the condition of their flattened car. They each took a shower and changed into their comfy clothes, thankful the quake hadn't affected anything in the valley.

A couple hours later, the front doorbell rang; Ali went

to answer it and was pleased to see Zach, DJ and Christine on the other side.

"Hey! What are you guys doing here?" She hugged each in turn.

"Well, my parents are out of town," Zach informed her.

"No one cares if I'm home or not," was Christine's reply.

She turned to DJ who simply said, "I just missed you."

"Mom! We have company!"

Caden walked into the room and shook hands with everyone. Lanie offered to make everyone lunch which was greatly appreciated. The girls went into the kitchen to help out and gossip.

The kitchen always served as the chatting spot where at any time, on any day, there would be a pot of coffee made, which would be drunk during homework help, future planning or quiet reflections.

Christine was filling Lanie in on her college plans, when Zach came in and started going through the cabinets.

"Sure, go ahead and make yourself right at home." Ali snorted.

"Don't mind if I do." Zach grabbed for a soda bottle and began to drink out of it.

"Excuse me, young man. Here we use these things called glasses." Lanie smirked while pointing to the appropriate cabinet. "And don't think that I haven't heard about that little speech of yours from Friday night either."

"Aw, Ms. Morgan, he didn't mean anything by it," DJ offered, as Zach began to defend himself while Lanie goodheartedly ribbed him.

Everyone sat around watching TV, snacking and dozing. That's what made the Morgan residence such a great spot, as long as you weren't doing something you weren't supposed to be doing, Lanie let you be.

"Do you guys want to do something tonight?" DJ asked the group as the sun began to set.

"Sure, I'm down!" Ali piped up.

Caden said he would call Gemma and a few others to see if they wanted to go and of course Zach and Christine were up for it.

"Cool, should we go to the movies? Out to eat? The pass?" Christine perked up with the thoughts of making plans.

Ali shrugged and gestured towards her mom. "Mom, is it okay for us to go out tonight?"

She nodded 'yes' while paging through her latest book. "But stay close to home."

They took a few minutes to decide on a time to meet up at Freddy's, then the others retreated back to their homes to get ready for the evening.

After the house was quiet again, Lanie turned on the news; the quake was all that anyone was talking about. Every news station had found an 'expert' to share their viewpoint of the earthquake and what may have caused it. Every theory from Global Warming to the Apocalypse was being aired on national television.

"Mom, are you taking any of this seriously?" Ali asked, as she walked through the family room to the kitchen.

"Nah, I just find Anderson Cooper extremely sexy." Lanie threw her daughter a saucy wink.

"You do realize that he's gay right?" Ali laughed.

"I know, I know," Lanie took a sip from her coffee mug. "But I figure that just means that if I can't have him, no other woman can either. And that's just fine by me." She smiled.

"What am I going to go with you, Mom?" Ali shook her head and walked down the hall to her brother's room. She knocked on the door until she got the usual harrumph, letting her know that he was awake.

She checked her cell and groaned when she saw that there were still no signal bars.

"What did you guys decide to do tonight?" Lanie asked, as she watched Ali apply her make-up.

"We're still not totally sure." Ali expertly glided the black kohl against the lid of her eye, knowing her mom wished she would use something lighter to bring out the color of her eyes. "But we'll keep it close; probably just hang out at Freddy's," she added so her mom would know that she was listening earlier.

"Okay, that makes me feel better with the cells down."

That was one downfall about modern technology,

everyone had a cell phone, but without a working tower it was pretty much pointless.

Ali heard the doorbell ring and silently cursed. She flicked the mascara wand twice on her lashes, smoothed on some gloss and pinched her cheeks the way her grandma had shown her how when in a rush.

She heard muted voices, then her mom's rich laugh carry down the hall.

"Stop hitting on my mother, DJ," Ali teased, as she stepped into the living room.

"Leave him alone," Lanie teased back, hugging them both. "And you, young man, keep her safe."

DJ smiled at Lanie and then at Ali.

"I promise."

CHAPTER FOUR

They pulled up to Freddy's and were surprised to see how empty the lot was.

"Wow, they are usually pretty busy on Sunday nights," Ali pointed out, climbing out of DJ's car. "Guess the quake spooked people more than we thought."

They walked into the restaurant, waved at Freddy, the owner, and claimed their usual tables. After a few minutes everyone started to arrive. Zach and Christine walked straight to the jukebox before joining their friends at the table.

Caden had gotten a ride with Gemma, who had invited Michelle and Bobby to join them again. Ali didn't know much about them except that Bobby played as a backup on the team, and he normally didn't hang out with anyone outside the gym. Michelle was a cheerleader like Gemma.

Ali always saw the three of them walking to classes together, sometimes joined by Caden if he had the class too or if it was in the same part of campus.

Despite the lack of patrons, they had a great time ordering large appetizer platters and sharing with each other. Zach put his last quarter into the box and selected

Jay-Z's *99 Problems*. The guys rapped along and the girls laughed at their silliness. Ali didn't want the night to end.

"So, are we heading to the pass or what?" Caden asked with his mouth full.

"That is disgusting!" Gemma shrieked, bringing herself, Michelle and Bobby into the conversation.

"We promised our mom that we would stay close to town," Ali began, eyeing Caden to back her up.

"Don't be such a worrywart, Ali; it's only ten minutes from here." Her brother finished off his milkshake, then reached for hers. "We'll be back in time."

Ali gave him a reproachful look and looked at DJ to speak up. DJ just shrugged his shoulders as if to say the decision is up to her.

"Okay," she sighed, "but just for a little bit." Everyone threw in a few bucks to cover the bill and then left a modest tip. Christine asked Ali and DJ if they wanted to ride with them and leave his car in the lot, but they declined not wanting to have to rush anyone not ready to leave to make the curfew.

DJ adjusted the vents, turning the heat onto low; he

popped in an old CD of classical music and it played quietly in the background.

"Sure you want to go? My parents are gone for the night and we could test out those condoms your mom gave you." DJ wiggled his eyebrows at her.

Ali laughed. "You are just a big ball of hormones, aren't you?"

They made the quick drive and DJ parked the car on the side of the road, opened his door and then walked around to open hers. She grabbed his outstretched hand for support, but he surprised her by pulling her into him and passionately kissing her. When he pulled back, Ali's eyes were still closed and her breathing was uneven.

"I don't think I'm alone," he said, his voice thick with desire. His lips laid feather light kisses against her throat before gently capturing her ear. She used her free hand to trail down his chest, to his waist, and was about to cup him when she heard Christine call her name.

"That girl has the worst timing in the world," DJ whispered into her ear.

Ali let out a small sigh before turning towards Christine. From the look on both her friends' faces, she knew she had interrupted. "Oh man." For once, Christine's over the top personality seemed to deflate. "I'm sorry."

And even though Ali was a little steamed, she couldn't stand to see that look on her face. Linking arms with her and DJ, they walked towards the fire pit, teasing her along the way.

Even though it was the same people from two nights before, the chemistry of the evening just felt off. Ali looked around at the different groups and could only describe it as "us vs. them." Sitting with her was Christine, Zach and DJ. Forming the other group were Gemma, Michelle and Bobby. Caden once again acted as the bridge between the two groups.

"So, have you given anymore thought about going to school at the U of A, sis?" Caden casually asked.

"Caden, give her a break already." DJ rolled his eyes.

"No, it's okay; I got another letter yesterday that has me changing my mind," Ali replied coyly.

"Where's this school at? Germany?" Caden grumbled out.

Ali just glared at him before replying, "Actually, it's a lot closer than that, jackass." Before he could say another word, Ali continued on, "While getting accepted to Spelman was an extreme shock and a great honor, I have other options to look at now."

She looked DJ straight in the eye. "Like the U of A." Everyone's head snapped up and a round of cheers began.

"I realized that I don't have to go halfway across the country to figure myself out!" She yelled over the din.

A few more minutes passed with everyone talking at once about which classes they wanted to take, who should room with whom or if it would be possible to find an apartment big enough for everyone to share.

Ali glanced over her shoulder and saw that Gemma, Michelle and Bobby were having their own intense discussion and nudged Christine's foot. She nodded her head in their direction and raised an eyebrow. Christine took a quick glance and shrugged, rolling her eyes.

"Hey, Gemma, have you heard from any schools yet?" Ali asked to bring them into the conversation.

"Um, no… I haven't applied," Gemma answered, looking at her friends for help.

"Oh," was all that Ali could think to say. The silence was heavy between them, searching for something else to talk about, she blurted out the first thing that came to mind. "Where you guys okay during the earthquake?" Ali asked Michelle and Bobby.

They glanced at each other, then at Gemma, before replying, "What earthquake?"

"How could you guys not feel the quake?" Christine asked. "Or even hear about it? It's been all over the news all day!"

Michelle shrugged and tossed her light brown hair over her shoulder. Before this evening Ali never noticed how much she and Gemma resembled each other. "I don't know what you're talking about. So Gemma, did you have a chance to check out that new store in the mall?" Gemma and Michelle went off on their own tangent with Bobby shrugging and staring off into space again.

DJ and Zach gave each other a questioning look. Caden glanced at his sister and Christine shook her head.

❧

It was getting close to curfew and Ali didn't want to be late and give her mother any more undue worry. "You guys ready to pack it in or are you going to hang out longer?" Ali called out to Christine.

"What are you guys doing?"

"We promised our mom we would be home by ten and it's getting close. Plus, we have school tomorrow," Caden said.

"Ugh, don't remind me. I have a paper due fifth period and I haven't even started it yet," Christine complained.

"Hey," DJ said, looking around. "Where did Michelle and Bobby go?"

Over the past hour, they had been able to sneak off without anyone noticing.

"They're probably taking advantage of the empty parking lot." Gemma shrugged, as she tossed trash into the bin. Once all the trash had been collected and tossed, everyone walked towards the lot, talking about the upcoming school week.

When they reached the lot, Bobby and Michelle where indeed taking full advantage of the empty lot and seemed unbothered by their various degrees of undress.

Shaking their heads, Ali and DJ waved goodnight and

said their goodbyes after Caden declined riding with them in favor of spending more time with Gemma.

DJ turned the key in the ignition and began to adjust the vents so the cold air wasn't blowing in their faces. He turned on the headlights and then the earth began to move.

***

Ali could hear the others let out startled screams while she held on tightly to the dash. This quake was so much worse than the one from the night before. Out of the windshield, Ali watched in horror as a divide began to take form, snaking its way towards the parking lot.

She tried to open the door, to run to the others but DJ's iron grip wouldn't let her go. Thick dust filled the air and she could no longer see anyone, all she could do was wait and pray that everyone was alright.

The shaking finally started to slow down and Ali wrenched her arm out of DJ's grasp. Throwing the door open, she barely heard DJ yell out to be careful before she called out, "Caden!" She inhaled some of the dust and it made her cough. "Christine!"

She heard DJ coming up behind her, but kept moving

forward. "Caden!" she coughed out.

"Ali, stop!" DJ caught her by the elbow, forcing her to slow down. "Stop," he coughed out. "You don't know where that crack is."

Ali struggled against DJ's hold, needing to find her brother and her friends.

"Ali!" Christine called back to her.

"Chris!" Ali nearly broke down with relief in hearing her friend's voice.

"Don't move," Christine coughed, "we're coming to you!"

Ali stopped struggling against DJ. The dust was settling and Ali could see the crack more clearly. It ran horizontally along the parking lot, destroying anything that was in its path.

"Ali!" She heard Caden calling.

"Caden, over here!" She held up her arms and waved them wildly around.

DJ grabbed his flashlight from the car and took her hand.

They carefully made their way into the lot, ensuring to point the beam ahead of them so not to stumble into the crevice. She saw Christine and the others standing a few yards away and ran for them.

"Oh my, God." Chris threw her arms around Ali when she got close enough.

"It's okay, we're okay," Ali soothed her.

Caden stumbled up to them and hugged both girls. Gemma had her arms wrapped around herself, and as they stood there, examining each other, they realized that Bobby and Michelle were not standing with them.

They all turned towards the lot where Gemma's car had been parked; nothing there now but a gaping hole. The guys pushed the girls back as they ran to the opening in the earth and looked down.

"I can't see anything," Zach yelled out.

"Here." DJ tossed him his flashlight. Zach shined the flashlight into the hole and let out a low groan. There in the stream of light they saw the taillights of Gemma's Honda.

"Bobby!" Caden called down. "Michelle!"

No one answered.

"We have to get them out of there!" Gemma cried, trying to push herself forward.

DJ grabbed her and pushed her back towards Ali and Christine.

"We're going to try, Gemma," he told her. "But we need to be smart and figure it out. We don't want anyone else getting hurt." DJ looked at Caden and Zach for help.

"Zach, do you have any rope in the truck? Or something that we could use to make one?"

Zach shook his head no.

"Human ladder?" Caden suggested. "At least this way we can see if they are okay and let them know that we're going to get help."

DJ and Zach nodded in agreement.

"Zach, no." Christine reached out for him.

"It's okay, babe."

Ali took Christine by the hand and led her over to Gemma; the three girls huddled together tightly support. DJ held the flashlight steady as Zach crawled to the edge of the hole.

"I hope your grip is as tight as it was at the game," Zach nervously joked.

"Brotha, please," Caden muttered. "No better hands, bro," he said as he sat on the ground and gripped Zach's ankles as he slowly lowered himself into the hole.

"Alright, DJ, shine the light."

DJ stood above Caden, holding the flashlight steady. Zach's entire body was nearly swallowed into darkness, when he began shouting to be pulled back up. DJ dropped the light and rushed to give Caden a hand.

"Well?" Gemma asked, tears streaming down her face.

Zach's face was as pale as a ghost's. "We need to get out of here." Zach grabbed Christine's hand and pulled her towards the truck.

"But what about Bobby and Michelle?" Gemma asked as Caden pulled her towards DJ's car.

"They can't be helped," Caden replied curtly, while she tried to pull away.

"What do you mean they can't be helped? They're…"

She couldn't bring herself to finish the sentence.

Caden and Zach looked at each other, "No they're not… I mean… not exactly." Zach stumbled, not knowing how to answer the question.

"What do you mean, not exactly?" Gemma narrowed her eyes.

Caden took a deep breath and stepped forward.

"When DJ flashed the light into the car, we saw… something."

Ali turned her head towards DJ and saw him run his hand through his short hair.

"What do you mean 'something?'" Gemma stood in front of Caden, demanding his attention.

"Babe, we don't know," Caden began.

"What in the hell did you see!" Gemma screamed out in frustration. "Just tell me!"

The guys took one last look at each other before DJ stepped up.

"There's something else in that hole, Gemma." He held up his hand when she tried to speak. "We don't know what it is, but we can't get to them."

Everyone stood around in silence as those final words kicked in.

"Look," Zach said, "we don't know how stable the ground is and we need to go and report this."

As if as on cue, the ground began to shake again, everyone holding on to each other to keep their balance.

Looking over her shoulder, Ali saw something rising from the split in the earth. A thick, dark liquid quickly bubbling up from its depths.

"Is that what you saw?" Ali whispered, pointing her finger.

"Ay Dios mio," Christine whispered.

The ooze was black as ink and bubbling like tar as it moved towards them.

"Stay back!" Zach yelled out, pushing Christine and Ali behind him.

Ali looked around his slender frame and let out a tiny scream, slowly climbing out of the hole, covered in ooze, was Bobby and Michelle.

CHAPTER FIVE

"Michelle?" Gemma took a few steps towards her friend. "Michelle, what happened?" Gemma was reaching out for her, not believing her eyes.

Michelle and Bobby were naked, their faces blank as they walked with a slow limp.

"Are you okay? How did you get out?" Again Michelle did not answer, they stayed at their pace.

"Okay, this is getting creepy, cut it out!" Christine said, holding onto Zach.

Michelle and Bobby stopped suddenly, as if Christine's words had put up an invisible wall.

"This isn't funny," Ali scolded, "we thought you were in serious trouble." Suddenly Bobby whipped his head to face her.

"We must collect you," he whispered. He slowly turned his body and began to walk towards Ali and DJ.

"Collect? What are you talking about Bobby?" He didn't answer; he just continued to walk towards them.

"Bobby, stop it! You're scaring me," Ali pleaded, hiding

behind DJ now.

"We must collect you," Michelle repeated, slowly beginning to walk towards Gemma.

Gemma let out a small shriek and backed away, as Michelle reached out her hand, dripping with ooze. Caden and Zach glanced at each other and nodded; they each picked up one of the heavy rocks at their feet and flung them at Michelle and Bobby, catching them off guard, easily bringing them down.

"Gemma, let's go!" Caden called to her, but she wouldn't move. Muttering a curse under his breath, Caden charged forward and picked her up.

Ali and DJ ran for his car, while Zach honked for Caden and Gemma to get into the truck. Caden lifted Gemma into the bed, hitting the side of the truck signaling Zach to gun it.

"Go back, go back!" Gemma yelled, banging on the glass of the cab. "Go back! They're alive!" She tried to jump over the side of the truck, but Caden held her back with an iron grip on the bottom of the truck bed.

"They aren't alive!" Caden yelled at her.

"You were wrong." Gemma twisted around and began kicking at the window. "Go back! She's my best friend, go back!" She sobbed.

Caden tried to remain in control. "Gemma, I wasn't wrong, when I looked in your car that stuff was all over them!" He temporarily lost his grip for a second when Zach hit a bump, a moment that Gemma tried to seize to escape again. "Gemma, listen to me!" Caden begged.

"No! They climbed out! They're alive!"

The truck began to slow down and when they looked up, they saw that DJ had pulled his car off to the side of the road.

"What the hell was that?" DJ shouted, as he climbed out of the car, slamming his door.

"Maybe you guys made a mistake?" Ali asked. "Or maybe they're just playing a cruel joke on us?" She shook her head; they couldn't have just seen Bobby and Michelle rise from the dead.

"When Caden helped lower me down, they were covered in that shit. We didn't make a mistake," Zach said firmly.

"Looks that ooze is coming out of that hole. Michelle and Bobby are," Zach paused for a second at a loss, "in trouble. We need to get to the police and report this." He looked around at his friends and they all nodded in agreement.

"Okay, let's all head to the station and go from there."

⁂

The drive into town was quiet. Caden and Gemma sat in the back of DJ's car, as they followed Zach. Ali's mind raced as she tried to piece together everything that had happened over the past hour. Was it really just a bad joke or did two people really die and come back as... what? Zombies? Ali subconsciously let out a snort.

"I'm glad you're finding humor about something," Gemma snapped.

"Whoa, whoa, whoa." Caden took Gemma's hand. "I understand that you're upset, but Ali didn't do anything." Gemma let out a huff and turned her head to look out the window.

"I'm sorry, Gemma," Ali spoke up. "I'm not laughing, really I'm not." She took a deep breath. "I'm just tired and scared and have no idea what is going on." Before Gemma could respond, Ali broke down in tears. The adrenaline from earlier was gone, replaced with doubts and fears. Did they really see Michelle and Bobby? Or had it been some big elaborate hoax?

As they drove through the streets towards the police station, they saw that the earthquake had indeed reached the valley. Trees and their branches had toppled over, blocking roads, destroying houses and landing on cars, and setting off the alarms. People stood outside their homes, some crying, some clutching a loved one, some calling out for the missing.

From the back, Ali could hear Gemma whispering something under her breath. As they approached the police station, Ali recognized their mother's silver sedan parked in one of the slots.

Once the car was parked, Ali threw the door open and rushed inside. "Mom!" she called out, pushing through the crowd, looking for Lanie.

"I'm here!" Lanie called out, running towards her daughter.

Ali ran to her and pulled her into a hug. "Are you guys okay?" Lanie pushed herself back and looked over her daughter.

"Yeah, Mom, we are."

"Where's your brother?"

"Here, Mom!" She pulled her son into her arms and then examined him head to toe. "I was so worried about you two." Her voice thick with tears.

Everyone began to huddle around her; she hugged and examined them all, just as she had her own children. "I am so glad that you guys are okay," Lanie said, while wiping tears away from her eyes. "I didn't know what to do after that last quake."

She went on to explain about how the power had gone out and how the landline wasn't working either. "The only thing I could think to do was to come here to the police station," she finished. "And it looks like you guys had the same idea." Ali and Caden glanced at each other, while Zach stepped forward.

"Actually, Ms. Morgan, we came here to get some help."

Zach repeated the story, first to Lanie and then to the

Deputy on duty. Caden and DJ stepped in and helped when Zach's words faltered, while Ali and Christine sat with Lanie and Gemma, continuing to comfort her.

After two hours of speaking with the Deputy, mentally and physically drained, the group walked out of the station into the chilly night air.

"Alright, now," Lanie spoke up, taking charge of the situation. "Zach, why don't you take Christine home, and, DJ, you can drop Gemma off, then you two come back to our house since your parents are out of town." She held up a hand when Christine was about to argue. "I don't want anyone staying alone right now." Her tone was stern and warned against further argument.

"Okay, Ms. Morgan, but before we do that, shouldn't we go tell Bobby and Michelle's parents about what happened?" DJ asked. "I mean, they say that they won't have anyone to do it until morning."

Lanie realized that they were right. "Alright, you guys go ahead, then straight back to my house?" She looked around at everyone, "Okay?"

Ali and Caden hugged their mom one more time and promised to come straight home.

"There's absolutely no point in asking you two to come with me, is there?"

Ali looked into her mom's eyes and saw the strain that the past few hours had created. "We'll be careful, Mom, promise."

They came to a stop outside a small, neat adobe house. The yard had received minimal damage, the only thing that truly looked out of place was the toppled over garden gnome.

The smell of burning wood and the lights shining brightly in the window indicated that someone was home, and even though none of them spoke it, they were all wondering how they were going to get through this once, let alone twice.

They all gathered in front of the wrought-iron gate leading to the front door. Taking a deep breath, Ali and Christine led the way down the walk. Before they reached the front door, it swung open, with Bobby's father standing there.

"Morning, Mr. McCobo," DJ began.

"Hey kids, kind of late for you to be out and about, isn't it?" the man asked them as they reached the door.

"Yes, sir, I guess it is," Zach agreed nervously, "but we have something to tell you." Mr. McCobo waved them into the small living room gesturing to the couch as he sat down in a recliner.

"Okay, what's up?"

Ali took a deep breath, "I am so sorry, Mr. McCobo," she began, tears welling in her eyes.

"Whoa, whoa, what's up with the water works?" He stood up and reached for the Kleenex box on the table besides her, handing it to her.

"Thank you," Ali muttered, as she tried to pull herself together. "We wanted to come here and tell you about Bobby before the police came."

Mr. McCobo jumped out of his chair. "What? What did he do?" he demanded. "Bobby, you get your butt out here right now!"

"Mr. McCobo, that's just it, he can't," she trailed off, letting out a gasp when Bobby walked into the room.

"What did you do, Bobby?" Mr. McCobo demanded. "Why are the police coming here?"

"I didn't do anything!" Bobby replied, throwing up his hands. "Honest!"

"But, but, you... and Michelle."

"What about Michelle?" Bobby whipped his head around at the mention of her name.

Christine and Ali looked at each other, and then looked at Bobby and his dad.

"You guys were trapped in the car, and covered in that ooze from the quake!" Caden blurted out.

"What are you talking about?" Bobby asked them, coming to stand next to his father. "I've been here all night." Bobby looked at his dad and Mr. McCobo nodded in agreement.

"But we saw you!" Christine accused. "We were at the pass and you scared the hell out of us, climbing out of that hole, talking about collecting people."

"For the last time," Bobby said in exasperation, "I haven't left this house."

Everyone was in stunned silence for a few moments before the questions started flying hard and fast. They questioned Bobby to the point that Mr. McCobo was sure that they were under the influence of something and threatened to take them all to the police station if they didn't knock it off.

"Just one more question," Ali began, but caught the look on Mr. McCobo's face out the corner of her eye. "Please?"

He let out a deep sigh, but nodded his head. "If you were here as you say you were, where's Michelle?"

Bobby began to shuffle his feet and roll his shoulders, looking around at everyone before answering. "She called me around eight o'clock, saying that her and her parents had to go out of town."

Ali tilted her head to the side and gave him a look that she hoped told him that she didn't believe any of it.

"We're sorry, Mr. McCobo." Zach stood up and reached out his hand. "We made a terrible mistake and will contact the police to let them know that Bobby is okay and at home."

Bobby's dad hesitated, but shook Zach's hand and

grunted his acceptance of his apology.

"You don't mind if we drive by Michelle's do you?" Christine asked Bobby as they walked towards the front door.

"Um, I don't see why," he said again, scratching his neck. "But if that will make you feel better, I can't stop you."

They said their goodnights and apologies as they walked out the door.

"We saw them!" Christine hissed.

"I know we did," Ali agreed.

"It just isn't possible," Christine groaned, as she leaned against the truck. "We s*aw* them… all Walking Dead style."

Gemma wanted to get to Michelle's as quickly as possible, to make sure that the house was empty and her friend really wasn't in some kind of terrible danger.

"Look, why don't you and Gemma go check on Michelle?" Zach said, throwing Caden his keys.

"I don't think we all need to go, and plus we need to figure out what to do about the police before they show up here."

Ali gave her brother a quick squeeze and told him to be careful before turning to Gemma. "I really do hope that Michelle is alright."

Gemma looked up at Ali and gave her a tight smile. "Thank you," she whispered, then cleared her throat. "And about earlier... I'm sorry."

Ali took her hand and gave it a quick squeeze.

Christine and Zach said their goodbyes and climbed into the back of DJ's car. DJ gave them a wave and then they were off. The streets were quiet, the steady drum of the tires was the only sound they heard.

"We saw them? Right?" Ali pinched the bridge of her nose. "I mean, Bobby and Michelle were at the pass?" She twisted in the seat and looked over the headrest. "But then what happened? How did Bobby get home?" Ali could feel a headache coming on.

"Let it go, babe," DJ muttered.

"What?" she said shocked, "how can you say that?"

"We had to be wrong." DJ shrugged, pulling into the driveway.

"Wrong?" Ali turned back in her seat to fully face him. "We were all wrong? All six of us, what? Just had the same exact hallucination at the same exact time?"

"Ali," Christine whispered in a cautious tone. "Let's get inside and get some coffee and clear our heads." She reached over the seat and placed her hand on Ali's shoulder. "We're exhausted and I think everyone is getting just a tad bit punchy." She cut her eyes over to DJ, silently telling him to be quiet.

"Let's get inside before your mom gets even more worried."

Ali shrugged Christine's hand off her shoulder and opened the car door. Without waiting for the others, she stormed up the walkway and opened the front door.

"Mom!" she called out. "Mom, we're home!"

"In the kitchen, baby!"

Ali walked towards the back of the house, the others following her there. As always a fresh pot of coffee was ready and waiting along with several coffee mugs.

"I figured you might need a cup after what you had to do." Lanie looked up from her laptop, her smile disappearing. "Where's Caden?"

Ali started to pass out the mugs. "He's with Gemma."
She held up her hand before her mom could get out the
next question. "Here, Mom." She filled a mug with coffee.
"You're going to need this."

CHAPTER SIX

Lanie sat slack-jawed as Ali finished recounting what had happened over the past hour. "Bobby, just came out of the room?" she asked, for the second time.

"Yep." Ali sighed as she took another sip of her coffee.

Lanie looked around at everyone gathered at the table. "And Michelle is supposedly out of town with her parents?"

"Yeah, that's what Caden and Gemma are checking on now."

"So, what happened at the pass?" She narrowed her eyes. "You didn't make a false report, did you?"

Ali couldn't believe her ears. First DJ and now her own mother. "I know what we saw, Mom," she said coolly. "We didn't make it up."

Lanie took another sip of her coffee.

DJ glanced at his watch and looked out the window. "Does anyone know where Michelle lives?" Christine and Zach shook their heads, while Ali shrugged.

"Maybe they're listed in the phonebook?"

Christine went to the pantry and grabbed the Yellow Pages. "Her last name is Edison, right?"

Ali nodded 'yes,' while reaching for the coffee pot when the ground began to shake once more. "Not again!" Ali's mug fell to the floor, as she clung to the counter.

"Get in a doorway," Lanie yelled "Now!"

Everyone scrambled for a door and held on to the frame as the quake rattled the house like a rag doll.

"Why isn't it stopping?" Christine yelled after a few minutes.

"I don't know!" DJ yelled back.

Ali looked at her mother and saw the fear in her eyes, and was sure it mirrored in her own. Caden was still out there.

❧

The shaking finally stopped and Ali ran to the front door.

"Ali, stop!" DJ and Lanie called out at the same time.

"I have to make sure Caden is okay." She suddenly felt that it had been wrong to let him go off with Gemma

90

alone.

"Ali." DJ grabbed her arm before she went outside. "We don't know where they went." He pulled her into him and held her tight. "Let's see if we can find Michelle's address in the phone book and then we'll go find them, okay?"

Ali squirmed while in his grasp for a moment, but stopped when the words sunk in.

"I'll grab the book," Christine whispered, as she walked back into the kitchen.

Ali went to her mother and wrapped her arms around her. "Mom, I am so sorry." She heard the tears in her voice and wished she sounded stronger.

"Sorry for what?" Lanie stroked her hair, pulling her in a little tighter.

"I should have gone with him, Mom."

Lanie shushed her daughter and rocked her as if she were a child again.

"No, honey, if you would have gone with him, then I would be twice as worried as I am now." Ali pulled back a bit to look at her mother; she nodded and wiped the tears from her eyes.

Zach and Christine walked into the living room and reported that they found the address for the Edison's. DJ grabbed his keys from the coffee table and gave Lanie a hug before taking Ali's hand.

"I'm sorry about before," he said. "I know that we all saw the same thing. I don't know why I said that."

She looked into his eyes and hesitated in answering.

"Ali," he whispered, "I'm really sorry."

She took a deep breath and nodded her head. "Let's go find my brother."

The last quake had left its mark throughout town.

"Man, Tucson is wrecked!" Zach exclaimed from the passenger seat.

Ali and Christine glanced out the back windows at the houses that had crumbled, trees that had lost several limbs or uprooted altogether, and the telephone poles toppled into the street.

DJ expertly maneuvered around the debris, driving down alleyways and side streets when their paths became too clogged. Police were on hand directing traffic, and Ali counted no less than seven ambulances' blaring by on their way to a call or hospital.

As they slowly progressed through town, she could also see families packing up their belongings and loading into cars.

"I wonder why everyone is leaving," Christine mused.

"Maybe, the houses have more damage than we see and they are going to hotels?" Ali offered, watching yet another family pile into their car getting ready to leave.

After waiting for yet another ambulance to pass, they finally reached the main road to Michelle's. The sudden shrill of Zach's cell phone startled everyone and he fumbled to get it out of his pocket. He took a quick glance at the screen. "Caden!"

Ali whipped her head forward, fingers digging into the headrest. "Where is he?" Ali bounced up and down in the backseat.

Zach waved at her to be quiet. "Caden, what's up? Wait? What? You're *where*?" Zach hit the dashboard and motioned for DJ to pull over. DJ pulled the car to the side of the road and tapped the steering wheel.

"Okay, okay, we'll be there soon." Zach motioned for DJ to turn around. "Caden? Hello, Caden? Ugh!" Zach looked at the blank screen and punched the dashboard.

"What's up, man?" DJ asked, as Zach told him to turn the car around.

"We have to go back to the pass," he told everyone.

"What? Why?" DJ asked.

"I don't know, that's all he got out before we were disconnected."

DJ flipped the car around in one fluid motion and headed back in the direction of the pass.

"What in the hell is he doing out there?" Ali questioned. "Is Gemma with him?"

Zach just shook his head. "I don't know, Ali."

Christine reached over and gave her hand a squeeze. "He's fine." Her voice was strong, but Ali didn't miss the tears welling in her eyes.

DJ decided to drive mostly on side streets to avoid the traffic jam now forming as others were fleeing from their homes. Ali silently willed DJ to drive faster and prayed that her brother was okay. They had just made it to a mile out from the pass, when DJ suddenly slammed on the brakes. Ali looked out the window shield and her blood went cold.

In front of them was a massive divide in the earth; thick black liquid came bubbling just below the rim of the crack. The road leading to the pass was cut off.

"How are we going to get there now?" DJ drummed his fingers against the steering wheel.

Ali resumed bouncing in her seat, as she tried to think of something. "We have to find a way, we have to find him." She looked around them and thought she saw something in the distance. "Look." She pointed to the north. "It looks like the opening gets smaller down that way."

DJ pressed down on the gas pedal, driving parallel against the opening. After a few minutes, they could make something out just ahead of them, a body lying on the ground.

"Oh no," Ali whispered, as Christine grabbed her hand.

"We don't know anything yet, babe." DJ met her glance through the rearview mirror. Before he could come to a complete stop, Zach flung the door open and ran to the body.

"It's him!" he called back to them.

Ali struggled to get out of the backseat, cursing the sleek two-door, as she pushed the seatbelt out of the way. Everyone else had gathered around him, but she found herself afraid to get close.

"Is he?" Ali whispered, suddenly feeling very cold, as she walked around them, reaching out a trembling hand to touch her brother. Just as she was about to touch his wrist, his hand grabbed hers and she let out a scream.

"Where am I?"

✤

Ali and Lanie were crying, hugging Caden tight in their living room, as he explained what had happened after they had left. Bobby and his father suddenly wanted to go out to the pass and see where he had supposedly met his demise. Caden couldn't understand the sudden need to go out there, but Bobby said that he thought it was funny and wanted to be in on the joke.

Caden had tried to convince them again that it wasn't a joke, that they had seen Bobby and Michelle in Gemma's car and how that car was in a crack in the earth out at the pass.

Mr. McCobo insisted that they go, to finally prove they were pulling a joke on them and it was getting old. He threatened to go to the police and report Caden and Gemma for making a false report for fun. They needed to go and see, once and for all, that he didn't believe them. It was time for this to be over.

"At that point, what could we do?" Caden slumped into the couch, placing an ice pack on his head.

"What happened next?" Lanie asked.

Caden continued his story, "I tried to talk them out of it, and I said there was no reason to go out there since they were obviously fine, but he just wouldn't let it drop." He told them that Bobby offered to take Gemma out there and on the way, stopped by Michelle's to show her that she really had left town. "I wasn't about to let her go off with someone I thought was dead!" He shook his head and looked at his mom. "We shouldn't have left that house."

"But, when Ali got home, she said that Bobby had been with his dad all night," Lanie told him, turning to look at her daughter.

"That's what he told us, Mom." Ali placed her head in her heads. "I mean, he wouldn't lie, would he?"

Lanie rubbed her back. "I don't know, baby."

"What happened next, C?" Zach asked.

Caden told Bobby that they would follow him and his dad to Michelle's house and once they were satisfied that Michelle wasn't there, they would go to the pass.

"Once we got to Michelle's, I don't remember anything after that."

"Well, I'm going to call the police and report this," Lanie announced, standing to go to the kitchen. "I can't believe that you kids would make a prank report, but it was definitely too far to lead you out on those false pretexts and then jump you. And where is Gemma? Lord, I hope she's safe."

The room was quiet for a few minutes, each caught up in their own thoughts.

"So, let me get this straight, Bobby and his dad *wanted* to go out to the pass?" Christine asked. "And then you go to Michelle's but end up at the pass and Gemma is gone?"

Caden just shrugged.

"Caden," Ali began gently.

"Look, I know what you're going to say, sis. I have no idea how I got there, one minute we were pulling up to the house and the next thing I know, you guys were standing over me."

Zach began pacing back and forth. "No. We didn't just find you, you called me."

Caden cocked his head to one side. "Dude, I didn't call you." He pulled out his phone and checked the screen. "No outgoing calls, and no signal." He threw the phone to Zach who flipped it open and saw he was telling the truth.

"But it was your number that came up, and I talked to you." Zach grunted out in frustration. "At least I thought it was you, it could have been Bobby."

"But why would Bobby do that?"

"I don't know what else to tell you." Caden stood and turned to his friends. "All I know is this: people I thought were dead are suddenly appearing alive. And my girl either helped them do this to me or is hurt somewhere."

Lanie walked back into the room, reporting that the

phones were still out.

"Well, you guys aren't going back out there," she stated flatly. "Enough is enough; it's time for the police to be brought in."

Ali and Caden looked at each other and then at their friends. DJ came and took Ali's hand.

"Mom," Ali began.

"Don't 'Mom' me! It's too dangerous and no one is leaving this house."

"Mom," this time it was Caden. "I am eighteen years old and I will leave to go find my girlfriend. I need to know what in the hell is going on."

Everyone froze. Neither of them had ever spoken to their mother that way and no one dared to make a sound now.

"I will be careful," he added more gently.

"We're going to back him up, Ms. Morgan," Zach spoke quietly, Christine and DJ nodding their agreement.

"Fine, but Ali--"

"I'm going too, Mom." Ali ignored the squeeze coming

from DJ. "I'm not letting Caden go without me."

Feeling resigned, she told them to be careful and to come straight back if they couldn't find Gemma at Bobby's or her home. Together, they would all go to the police and report her missing. Ali and Caden gave her a hug and told her to lock up tight, promising that they would be back as soon as they could.

Zach's truck was also missing, so they all piled into DJ's coupe, a little cramped, but doable.

"Which house first?" DJ asked, while starting the car.

The logical decision was to go to Bobby's house, since he lived closest. It was without much surprise that they found it to be empty.

As they drove in the direction of Gemma's house, they all noticed how quiet the streets where. Everywhere they looked, they saw the devastation of the quake. Power lines down, telephone poles tumbled over like dominos, cars lying beneath fallen trees.

"You would think people would be out, cleaning this stuff up," Zach remarked, as he tried to reposition himself with Christine on his lap. "No people, no police, no fire crews, this is just weird."

They continued to drive on in silence until they reached Gemma's house. The two-story stucco home looked untouched from the damage.

"Huh, doesn't even look like the quake made it this far," Christine noted, as they approached the front door, looking at the pristine yard.

Caden knocked on the front door and they stood waiting for an answer. After a few seconds, Caden tried again, still with no response.

"Is the door locked?" DJ asked, already reaching for the knob, turning it easily in his hand.

"Hello?" Caden called out. "Gemma? Mrs. Curtis? Mr. Curtis?" Caden took a few steps into the foyer and reached for the light switch.

The house stood quiet, only the faint hum of the fridge was heard. They walked through the family room to the kitchen; Caden heading upstairs to check things out, Ali opening the door leading to the garage. The Curtis's SUV was there, but there was no sign of the family.

"What in the hell is going on?" he asked, coming back downstairs, throwing his hands up in the air.

Christine walked over to the backdoor to check out the yard. "This is so weird," she muttered. "Every house on this street has some sort of damage, broken tree limbs, messed up flower beds, something. But this house looks like it hasn't been touched."

They walked back into the kitchen and leaned against the granite countertops.

"See? I told you there was something strange about this girl," Christine whispered.

Ali rolled her eyes at her and went to stand next to the sink. She was about to suggest that they head back to her house, when she heard a strange gurgling sound coming from the drain.

"Did you hear that?" she asked Christine.

"Hear what?" Ali turned the tap and after a few sputters and groans, a thick brown liquid began to flow.

"Huh, it looks like that stuff got into the water system."

"You're not going to drink that are you?" Christine asked, as DJ grabbed a glass from the counter and held it under the faucet, collecting about a cup.

"No, I just want a close up look at it." He held it up to

the light and slowly turned the glass around, examining the contents, before pouring it back out. "I don't know what that is, but Drain-O wouldn't have shit on it."

"Let's get going, no one's here." The look on Caden's face was enough to break Ali's heart. She went up to her brother and put an arm around his waist. "Don't worry, we'll find her and find out what happened."

Just then, they heard the front door open. Caden ran out of the kitchen with everyone right behind him. Once they reached the living room, their hearts stopped. Standing there, covered in blood, were Bobby and Michelle.

CHAPTER SEVEN

"What are you doing here?" Zach moved to the front of the group, gently pushing Christine behind him, even though she struggled to stand by his side.

"We came for you," Michelle answered in a chilling voice.

"Came for us? You're supposed to be out of town!" DJ moved to the side, with Ali behind him. She realized that the guys were slowly surrounding them and signaled to Christine to knock it off.

"We must collect you." Bobby took a step forward and moved toward Caden.

"This isn't funny anymore. Knock it off!" Christine yelled at them.

"We must collect you," Michelle said again, reaching for Ali.

"Don't touch me!" She slapped Michelle's hand away.

"We much collect you," they repeated in unison.

"You ain't collecting shit." Caden went to tackle Bobby, but missed when Bobby side-stepped at the last minute.

"We must collect you," Michelle said, still in that voice that sent shivers down Ali's spine. "Or kill you."

Christine looked around Zach. "Kill us?" It was as if their minds had finally finished processing the blood on their clothes.

"Bobby... Michelle, what did you do?" Ali whispered, her eyes growing large as Michelle slowly approached them.

"Bobby's dad didn't conform," she said, her voice calm, as if she was discussing the weather. "We must collect you."

Before anyone could blink, Bobby lunged for Ali again. Caden cold-cocked him with a right hook. "Backdoor?" Ali breathlessly suggested.

"Um, that may not be an option," Christine squeaked.

Everyone turned towards the door and Ali let out of a small scream; standing at the backdoor were Gemma and her parents, wearing the same blank expression as Bobby and Michelle.

"Gemma?" Caden took a step towards her.

"We must collect you." Michelle reached out her hand and moved towards Caden.

As they inched closer, they heard the backdoor glass break. Mrs. Curtis had broken the glass with her hands, blood trickling from the gashes on her fists. "We must collect you."

They were now surrounded.

"What are we going to do?" Ali whispered.

"The garage." DJ motioned. "Get to the garage."

"Gemma," Caden whispered.

"Let's go, C." Zach urged.

"No." Caden stepped in the front of the group and rushed to Gemma.

"No!" Ali cried out, but before she could break away from DJ, she saw that Gemma had stepped in front of her parents.

"Run!" she yelled, pushing her mother into her father and throwing them off balance sending them to the ground. She grabbed Caden's hand and pulled him to the door that led to the garage.

Zach threw a chair at Bobby and Michelle, grabbing Christine with Ali, and DJ just a few steps behind.

Once inside the garage, the boys barricaded the door.

"What is going on, Gemma?" Christine yelled, grabbing her.

"Christine!" Ali yelled, breaking her grip.

"I don't know! One minute I'm with Caden, the next minute I'm at Bobby's house," her voice dropping to barely a whisper, "watching my parents kill his dad."   .

Christine's face was full of rage. "And we're supposed to believe you?" Christine shouted, "¡Usted hembra loca, mentirosa!"

Ali agreed that one of them was acting crazy, but she wasn't sure it was Gemma at that moment. Christine was about to grab her again, when the banging on the door drew her attention.

"We have to leave. Are there keys for this thing?" Zach asked, pushing the door shut along with Caden.

"Yeah, there's an extra set in the lock box." Gemma ran to the other side of the garage and pushed in a code to open the small box. "Here." She threw the keys to DJ who unlocked the doors.

Christine, Ali and Gemma climbed into the back.

"Come on, guys!" DJ shouted out the door.

Caden and Zach nodded three times and then broke for the truck. The door burst open and Bobby fell to the ground.

"Hold on," DJ cautioned, as he pushed the garage door opener.

"What are you waiting for? Floor it!" Gemma urged.

"But... what if someone is behind us?"

"Then I will feel really bad about doing this." Zach stepped down on DJ's foot and the Yukon crashed through the half raised garage door.

Michelle and Mrs. Curtis's screams shattered the stillness of the night, as the truck rolled over them. DJ's foot faltered at the sound.

"Floor it!" Gemma yelled.

With a quick look through the rearview, he stomped down on the gas.

"Oh my God. Oh my God. Oh my God." Gemma was rocking herself between Ali and Christine.

DJ's hands where visibly shaking on the wheel. Ali closed her eyes but opened them immediately, not wanting to see Michelle's lifeless body lying in the driveway.

"What is going on?" Christine whispered as tears ran down her face.

The question was met with only silence. As they turned the corner, they saw a crowd surrounding something.

"Oh, thank God, help," Ali whispered from the back.

"Ummm, I don't think so, Ali." Zach pointed.

At the sound of the car's engine, the crowd turned. Lying on the ground, they could make out an elderly couple, covered in blood and not moving. The crowd descended on the truck, banging on the windows, pulling at the door handles.

"Go, DJ, go!" Caden yelled.

DJ threw the truck in reverse, smashing into a fence, as he turned the truck around.

"Mom," Ali whispered, grabbing Caden's arm. "We

have to go get Mom."

A few minutes later, they pulled up to the Morgan residence; everyone jumping out and running inside.

"Ms. Morgan?" Zach called out.

"Mom!" Caden ran down the hall and checked the rooms and the bathroom. "She's not here," he announced, running back to the living room.

"She has to be here, she wouldn't have left without us." Ali ran back to the kitchen and let out a blood-curdling scream.

There was Lanie lying in the doorway, lifeless, blood covering the left side of her face.

"Who could have done it?" Ali sobbed, holding her mother's body. "Who?"

DJ kneeled down beside her, wiping away the tears to make room for more. Christine sat on her other side, resting her head on her shoulder.

"I don't know, baby," Christine began, her voice turning cold, "but I have a feeling Gemma could tell us."

Gemma's blonde head snapped up at the accusation. "I

don't know anything!"

"Oh, yeah? Then why were you so hell-bent on following Bobby and his dad to the pass? You knew that Caden wasn't going to let you go off by yourself with those two!" Christine stood up and moved to stand over Gemma.

"Not after what we saw, and then we just happen to find you with your killer parents and friends, telling us that you *just* happen to wake up in Bobby's home and watch them kill his dad?" Christine continued to stand over her, becoming more enraged by the passing second. "Then what? Did you all come here? And if you did, give me one damn good reason not to kick your lily white ass right this second!"

Zach grabbed Christine and pulled her to him. Ali looked up at Gemma, anger flashed in her grey-blue eyes.

"Well? Was it here? Was it you or your mom or your dad that killed our mother?" Everyone looked at Ali, astonished. "You wanted to go to Michelle's to make sure she was really out of town." Ali clenched her fist and kept Gemma locked in her gaze. "But you didn't go to Michelle's; you went along with Bobby and his dad's idea. You went back to the pass." Ali had Gemma backed into a corner.

"What did you do to my brother?"

Gemma flinched at the mention of Caden, and then squinted in anger. "Are you kidding me? Are you *kidding* me?" She jumped back at Ali's face.

"You aren't the only one that lost a parent today. I don't know what happened, you selfish bitch, and I really don't care if you believe me!"

She turned on her heels and stormed out the front door with Caden closely following.

"Anyone else notice that she didn't answer the question?" Christine asked.

A few seconds later, Caden came back into the house. "There are more of them out there right now."

Zach and DJ hurriedly turned off the lights and made a makeshift door to secure the back.

"We need to move, and we need to move now." Ali ran down the hall and grabbed her duffle bag, along with a picture of her and her mother taken during the past year.

"Where are we going?" she asked, as she reentered the

room.

"Good idea, sis," Caden commented, when he saw her carrying the bag. He ran down the hall to his room to grab some clothes.

"I guess we can try my house," Zach offered. "My parents are out of town, remember?"

While they waited a few minutes for Caden to grab a few of his things, Ali and Christine moved slowly around the kitchen, gathering up water, sodas and snacks to put in the truck.

"Okay, let's get going." Caden took another look around the small living room, where hours ago, he had pretty much thought that things couldn't get any worse.

"Let's go, C." Ali gently pulled him to the door.

With dawn quickly approaching, the others had already snuck into the truck. Ali took a quick look around the yard and with a nod to Caden, they silently walked to the SUV.

"Keep a close eye on her," Christine whispered into Ali's ear, as Caden steered the SUV out of the driveway. Ali nodded in agreement; it just didn't add up.

Caden being left near the split where this mess began,

Bobby and Michelle trying to 'collect' them, Gemma... her parents.

What was her deal? Ali didn't know, but she was determined to find out. As they slowly drove through the streets towards Zach's house, they continued to see people walking as if in a trance. They realized that if they didn't draw too much attention to themselves, they were left alone. If Caden accidentally gunned the engine, the crowd would turn on them and begin to pound on the windows and try to open the doors.

Ali leaned into DJ's warmth and quietly cried, remembering certain things about their mother. Like the time she took them to the zoo when they were six and brought them both an ice cream cone. Ali couldn't recall exactly what she was doing, but her ice cream fell from the cone and she began to cry.

Caden and her mom came running to her to make sure she wasn't hurt. While her mom comforted her, promising a new ice cream, Caden gave half his scoop to her. They had always been there for each other.

"Oh, DJ, we weren't there for her. I wasn't there for her." She reduced to tears again and DJ pulled her closer.

"Sis, don't think that way," Caden soothed from the driver's seat. "If we had known, we wouldn't have left her."

She could tell from the thickness in his voice, he was fighting back tears too. They rode in silence the rest of the way until they got to Zach's. When they arrived they couldn't believe their eyes.

The beautiful ranch style home had been vandalized. Windows broken, the front door hung by one hinge, the flower beds trampled.

Zach let out a sigh. "At least I know my parents are safe." He gasped and quickly looked at Ali and Caden.

They gave him a small smile, encouraging him to go.

"Chris, stay here," he said firmly, as he opened the door.

She rolled her eyes and began to follow.

"No." He pushed her back into the truck. "Please, just listen to me?"

Zach pleaded. Christine stopped short, and nodded. He shut the door and knocked on the driver's side window. "C, two minutes. If I'm not back in two minutes, go." He tuned out Christine's protest and walked through the front door.

Slowly, he entered the house, listening for anyone or anything that didn't belong. He ventured further inside, each beat of his heart pounding in his ears. As he neared the kitchen, he heard a licking sound.

"Cisco?" Zach called out, calling his pup. The licking soon turned to a whimper. "Cisco?" Zach kneeled down to check on the pug, reaching out to pet him.

Cisco turned towards his master and lunged for his throat. Zach screamed, blocking the dog with his forearm. The dog's eyes were wide and his hackles raised.

"Cisco, stop!" Zach yelled at the dog, but he didn't listen, it crouched on its hind legs, ready to attack again.

"Zach!" Christine yelled, as she ran through the door.

"Get out of here!" Zach yelled back, stumbling to get back on his feet.

Upon seeing a new threat, Cisco bared his teeth, foam forming around his mouth.

"Cisco!" Zach called to get the dog's attention; Cisco whipped his head side to side, trying to decide on whom to attack first.

"Cisco!" Christine called. "Come get me, you son of a bitch!"

Cisco pounced at Christine, and then gave out a yelp of pain. Bright red blood ran down Christine's arm as Cisco lied on the floor.

"Are you alright?" Zach ran up to her, examining every inch, looking for the source of the blood.

In her right hand, she held a small blade. "I'm okay," she said, as she wrapped her arms around Zach. "Are you okay?" Christine held him at arm's length and gave him the same once over he gave her.

"I'm fine." He held her close again. "Let's hurry." Zach ran down the hall to his room and grabbed some clothes, throwing them into a bag, as he rushed back to Christine. Just as they reached the front door, they heard Caden begin to honk the horn.

As they ran back outside, they saw a new crowd quickly approaching them. Zach pushed Christine into the truck and jumped inside.

"I thought I told you to leave without me?" Zach yelled

at Caden, as he backed out of the drive.

"Have you met your girl?" DJ asked, as he held onto the handlebar and braced for the quick shift into drive.

"She said that she would cut off my balls if I left without you," Caden called over his shoulder, "and by the look of whatever messed with her, I made the right choice."

"It was Cisco," Christine said in a small voice, suddenly shaking. "He was attacking Zach."

"It wasn't him, Chris; I don't know what got into him." Zach said, as he shook his head. "Wait, he was licking water from his bowl…" His voice trailed off.

"Mind filling us in?" Gemma asked and again something seemed off with her voice.

By Zach's delayed response, Ali thought he sensed it too.

"What did you miss?" Christine snapped. "He went in, the dog went crazy and attacked him and now the dog is dead."

"Well, excuse me, I was just trying to get the whole story," Gemma snapped back. "I need to gather."

Gemma's eyes got wide and she clamped her mouth shut.

"You need to gather what?" DJ asked.

"Nothing, I didn't mean… I mean," Gemma began to stutter.

"Gemma, what do you mean 'gather? '" Caden reached over to her.

"Stop the car!" Gemma suddenly screamed, scaring Caden into slamming on the brakes. She reached for the door handle.

"Oh no, you don't!" DJ yelled at her, trying to grab her arm. When he touched her arm, he pulled his hand back, feeling as if he had been burned. "What the hell?" he asked, as he rubbed his hand.

"Let me out."

Everyone froze at the sound of Gemma's voice.

CHAPTER EIGHT

No one spoke as they looked at Gemma, who no longer sounded like a seventeen year old cheerleader, but sounded like a gruff and grizzled truck driver.

"I said, let me out. Now." She placed her hand over the locking mechanism of the door handle and everyone heard a soft click. She turned to face Caden. "Sorry, baby, I wanted this to work out differently." Her voice was once again normal. She looked at everyone else, giving them a saucy wink. "I'll catch you guys later."

With that, she opened the SUV door and walked into the angry crowd that had gathered around them. As she raised her hand, they fell back and began to kneel.

"What the hell..." Zach's voice trailed off.

They watched as she stood before them, a queen in front of her subjects.

"Caden," Ali urged, "drive."

Caden's eyes were glued to the rearview mirror, continuing to watch as Gemma commanded the crowd that kneeled before her.

"Caden!" Ali yelled, snapping her brother out of his

trance.

"Right, sorry." Caden stepped down on the gas pedal, side swiping the car next to them as they drove away from the scene.

"Did that really just happen?" Christine whispered. "Did she just... lord over them, or something?" No one answered. "And what did she mean by 'catch you guys later?'" Zach asked.

Ali climbed into the front seat, careful not to knock into Caden. "I guess we know who took you back to the pass," she said softly.

"Yeah, but why?" Caden asked back.

They all just shrugged, realizing that they all had so many questions but no one to give them answers.

"Where do we go from here?" Ali asked. "Do we just leave the city? Should we try to get help?" Several seconds passed as everyone thought about what to do.

"Wait." Christine's voice rose in panic. "Nando! I need to see if I can find Nando."

Caden gave her a nod and they drove in silence for the rest of the way, absorbed in their own thoughts.

Occasionally they would come across a few people, all affected by the sludge.

"How did they drink that stuff?" Ali asked, watching, as they slowly moved past them, drawing little attention to themselves.

"The water must have been contaminated before it got thick. I remember giving Cisco fresh water before leaving last night," Zach remembered.

"But we've been…" Ali trailed off; her eye caught by the column of smoke rising from a few streets over. "Oh, no," she whispered. She mentally counted the houses and her heart dropped.

"Caden, hurry." Christine clutched the headrest.

Caden sped up and rounded the corner of her street.

"No, no, no," Christine moaned, looking at the shell that was left of her home. Several houses on the block where still burning, while others were burnt to the ground. "Stop the car!" she shrieked.

Caden slowed to a stop and Christine jumped out.

"Nando!" she yelled, running up the drive towards the front of the house.

Ali and Zach ran up the drive with her.

"Nando!" Christine yelled again, looking through a broken window, while Zach went to the backyard, returning quickly.

"There's more people back there. We got to go," he whispered, trying to pull Christine towards him.

"No! I'm not leaving without my little brother." She pushed him away and ran into the smoldering house.

"Chris!" Ali staged whispered, watching as her friend disappeared into the house and saw the backyard fence swing open. "Chris, they're coming!" Ali began to back towards the car, looking at Zach who nodded and ducked in after her.

"Christine, let's go!" Zach pleaded once more, before grabbing her arm.

"Let go of me!" She pushed him away, trying to shake him off, when she abruptly stopped struggling.

Walking towards them, with the same twisted look as the others that had been infected was Christine's mother. She came to a stop a few feet away from her daughter. Her stare was blank, blood covered her hands and ripped shirt.

"We must collect you," she whispered, reaching for her daughter.

Christine backed away, shying away from her touch. Zach wrapped his arm around her and pushed her behind him.

"Mistress, will be pleased. I will be rewarded."

Zach risked a quick look towards Christine, disgust written all over his face.

"Where's Nando?" Christine demanded, making her mother pause.

With a tilt of her head, she quietly regarded her daughter before she held up her hands. "He resisted," and a small squeal of delight escaped from her lips.

"You bitch!" Christine lunged at her, but Zach caught her.

"Come on, we have to go."

Christine kicked and punched, wanting nothing more than to hurt her mother. Zach picked her up and used her kicking to keep the other woman at bay and rushed out the house. The others who had been in the backyard turned in the direction of the commotion and began after them.

"Let me go!" she screamed, as Zach pushed her into the car.

"Hit me all you want, you're not going back there!" he yelled back. He had barely gotten himself into the truck, when Caden floored it, the force of the takeoff slamming the door shut, leaving Christine's home, mother and the nightmare far behind.

The silence was broken by a gut-wrenching sob from Christine. Ali had never seen her friend cry, much less hear the amount of sorrow coming from her now. Zach wrapped his arm around her, pulling her into his lap.

"Shh, baby, shh."

Christine grabbed his t-shirt, burying her face in his neck. Ali looked over to DJ, who had been in the back of the truck the entire time. He was looking out the window, completely detached from the scene unfolding right in front of him. Ali let out a small huff, as she turned back around in her seat. Caden threw her a questioning look; she just shook her head and looked out her own window, trying to give Christine as much privacy to grieve as possible.

Caden continued to drive around, not really sure where else to go. "Should we try your house? Just leave town? Try to get help somewhere else?" he asked, breaking the silence.

"Shouldn't we try the police station first?" DJ finally spoke up. "Maybe they have something set up as a safe house?"

"Now you want to offer help?" Ali spat out. "Where were you back there? Why didn't you try to help?"

DJ stared at her, his face still void of emotion.

"Fine, stay quiet." Ali shrugged, the emotions of the past couple days wearing her down. Christine had fallen asleep in Zach's arms, still clutching his shirt, so he merely shrugged in agreement.

Caden let out a long sigh. "To the police station we go."

The sun was beginning to set and all Ali could think about was finding a safe haven where they could rest and begin to truly process everything that had happened.

She let out a small snort when she realized that just two days ago her largest worry was about going off to college.

Her small smile turned into a frown when she thought about her mother. Why was it so important for her to go off and leave her mother behind? She could have found her independence just as easily at home.

"What's wrong, sis?"

Sometimes she wondered about Caden, usually so oblivious to her moods yet so perceptive, especially in the times when she wanted to keep her thoughts private.

"Just thinking about Mom."

He reached over and gave her hand a small squeeze. "I know," he said, his voice cracking. "Me too."

She returned the squeeze. "Are we doing the right thing?"

Caden gave her a puzzled look.

"By going to the station? Shouldn't we just get the hell out of here and try to find help somewhere else? Somewhere not affected by the quake?" She threw another glance at DJ, who had returned to looking out the window again.

"It can't hurt, can it?" Caden asked her back. "I mean, if no one's there, we'll head out." He lifted his hand from the steering wheel and checked the gas gauge. "We're good on gas, should at least be able to make it to Casa Grande if we head that way… or Green Valley." He trailed off, as he thought about which direction would be the right way to go.

Resigned, Ali sat back in the seat and prayed that DJ was right, that they were going in the direction of safety.

The soft glow of the police station lights shined like a beacon as they approached the building. Ali's discomfort slowly began to fade when she saw that patrol cars and other vehicles littered the lot, signaling that people were there and hopefully okay.

Caden pulled into the lot and parked the car next to the entrance. Once the engine was cut off, Caden removed the keys from the ignition.

"Wait," Zach said, reaching for Caden's shoulder. "Do you think that's such a good idea? What if we have to make a break for it?"

"No, we should be safe here," DJ reassured them. "Let's get inside and get some help."

Ali took a deep breath and opened her door. She watched as Zach helped Christine out of the truck, giving her a small smile and grabbing her hand once they were outside.

Christine leaned into Ali and they walked up the stairs to the front doors together. Zach reached out and pulled open the front door, only to find it locked.

"Ugh! You have got to be kidding me!" He began to bang on the door, rattling the handles.

"Maybe that's a good sign?" Caden offered. "Maybe it's locked to keep people inside safe?" He looked around the front of the building and saw the after-hours call button.

"Hold up, dude." He jogged over to the button and pressed it down. A few seconds later, a deputy came to the door, holding his weapon ready.

"Go away!" he shouted through the door.

"No! We need help!" Ali yelled back, pissed they were being turned away.

"We aren't letting anyone in, we aren't taking any chances!"

It was all too much. Her mother, Gemma, Christine's family, and the nagging feeling she had missed something important all day finally came crashing down.

"Listen!" she yelled. "We have been chased, family members have been murdered and my brother's girlfriend turned out to be their goddamn leader!" She walked closer to the door, her breath visible on the glass. "Either you let us in or I will break this glass and let everything in." Ali and the deputy stood facing each other, his gun still raised, level with her chest. "Either shoot me or stand back." Ali picked up one of the stone pavers that decorated the flower beds surrounding the entrance.

"Wait, wait!" he said, finally lowering his gun. "Come in." He took his keys out of his pocket and unlocked the door.

Ali dropped the slab and looked back at her friends. They all looked at her with a mixture of bewilderment and awe.

"Way to go, sis," Caden spoke up and stepped up to her, slapping her on the back.

DJ gave her a smile and took her hand, pulling her into the station. Once inside, the deputy relocked the doors and ushered them into the back. Ali's outburst had taken the last of what little energy she had left and she leaned into DJ's warmth and strength. She wasn't sure what was going on with him, but she was grateful for him now.

"Sorry about the gun, but I had to be sure you were okay." He gestured for them to enter a large conference room. Inside, there was already a small group of people gathered, some huddled in blankets, others holding cups of coffee or sodas.

"Can I get you folks some coffee? Juice? Blankets?" the deputy asked.

They graciously accepted his offer and he disappeared down the hall. Ali looked around, taking in the faces of those surrounding her: an elderly man, holding a cup of coffee and gazing into space, a family of four, trying to soothe their infant as their eldest asked endlessly when they could go home and a middle-aged couple, grasping hands and sharing a blanket, tears streaming down the woman's face. Then there was a single mother holding her young son and daughter close; singing softly to keep them occupied. Looking at them reminded Ali of their own mother and tears welled in her eyes. The deputy returned then, passing out blankets and bringing in a fresh pot of coffee.

"So, how did you guys get here?" he asked, leaning against the wall.

Ali realized that everyone's ears perked up at the

question and looked at Caden and DJ to answer. She leaned against DJ's shoulder, as she listened to him recount the events from earlier. She looked over at Christine and saw that she was also leaning into Zach for comfort. Caden sat between them, bridging the group, as usual. Once DJ was done, the deputy scratched his head.

"So this, Gemma... Curtis, did you say?" DJ nodded. "So she's the leader of this nonsense?"

Ali couldn't tell if the deputy was taking them seriously or not, and at that point, she didn't care. All she wanted to do was sleep.

"Yes, sir," Zach said, standing to stretch. "I know it sounds out there, but it's true."

The deputy scratched his head again. "Well, I can see that you guys are pretty beat." He turned to address the room as a whole. "We've set up cots in the other room and there are also the holding cells for people to use."

A few began to stand and move towards the cots. Ali looked around and Caden nodded towards the cells.

"Let the kids have the cots," he said.

Ali sleepily nodded and rose, once again taking DJ's

hand and let him lead her to the cell. Zach, Christine and Caden were right behind them.

As the others settled into the beds, Ali pulled DJ close. "I'm sorry," she said. "It's just… you've been so detached since we got to Christine's…"

Her apology was cut off by his kiss.

"Whoa, what was that for?" she asked.

"I love you," he whispered into her ear. "I didn't want to. I am just so, so sorry."

Ali pulled her head back and looked into his eyes, trying to understand what he was trying to say.

"DJ?" she asked, as he rose from the bed they sat on.

He gave her one last glance before walking to the cell door, and shutting it behind him.

☙❧

"What the hell, dude!" Zach yelled, rushing to the iron bars and trying to open them. "Let us out!"

Ali sat on the cot, stunned. Her, Caden, Zach and Christine were trapped in the cell.

"I'm so sorry," DJ pleaded to her. "I'm under orders."

She couldn't respond.

Thinking back to everything that had happened. DJ always being so calm when things were going wrong, his detachment from Christine and her brother and mother. Wanting to come to the police station.

"You wanted us to come here." Her throat going dry, barely making a whisper. "You wanted us to come to the police station."

Everyone stopped talking and stared at DJ.

"You set us up, man?" Caden asked.

DJ continued to stare at Ali, his face a hard mask, but his eyes trying to tell her something.

"I'm going to kill you!" Caden suddenly rushed to the bars and reached out to DJ, who merely took a step out of his reach.

He began to walk down the hall towards the conference room they had just left. From the cell next to them, they heard a small laugh escape from the little girl that so much reminded her of herself at that age. When she looked up, she was holding her blanket and a teddy bear close to her chest; she looked directly at Ali, her laughter bringing a twinkle to her eyes.

"We must collect you."

Ali stared at her, frozen.

"We must collect you all," she whispered, before lying back down with her mother and closing her eyes.

CHAPTER NINE

"Oh my God." Zach began pacing the small space. "We have got to figure out how to get out of here."

Christine began to shake; Caden placed a blanket around her and went to inspect the cell door again. While the guys were trying to find a way out, Ali sat on the bed, tears falling onto her lap.

How could I be so stupid? she thought to herself, *I knew there had to be a reason one of the most popular boys in school picked me, stupid, unassuming me.* She let out a small growl as her anger grew. Caden came and sat next to her on the bed.

"Don't be upset, Ali, I was tricked too."

She looked at her big brother and leaned into him. "Thanks, C." She then let out a sigh. "We're trapped aren't we?"

Christine came and sat on the other side of her.

"Don't you dare think that way! We're going to figure out how to get out of here." The old Christine was beginning to resurface and determination was written all over her face.

"We'll figure something out, we just have to think."

Zach finally stopped pacing and stood in front of them.

Ali looked around him to see if the little girl was still awake and listening to their conversation. "Okay," she whispered. "What are our options?"

Caden took her cue and lowered his voice. "We could call for the deputy," he began.

Christine shook her head. "We have to think that he's with them, I mean, why else would he let us in here?"

Zach nodded in agreement. "Yeah, I think we're pretty much on our own."

They remained silent for a few moments, then Christine had an idea. "What if I fake I'm sick? Then someone would have to open the door!"

"That's not a bad idea, babe." Zach reached for her hand and caressed her face with his other. "But then what?"

"Then you guys could jump whoever comes to check on us." Christine rolled her eyes at him. "After the way I was acting in the car, DJ won't be hard to convince."

Caden and Zach were whispering about what the other would do once someone came through the door.

"Hold on, guys," Ali whispered to get their attention. "If Christine pretends to be sick, that's going to raise a lot of noise." She motioned to the cell next to them, where the family was. "How are we going to get around all of them?" Ali knew instantly that she had just sunk their plan, but it was a possibility they had to face.

"Well, hopefully, the deputy will be the one to come check on her, since he has the keys," Caden offered. "Then Zach and I can overpower him and take his gun."

Ali knew it wouldn't be that simple, but they needed to do something. "Okay," she finally said. "What do I do?"

Christine was lying on the ground, moaning and shaking violently.

"Help! We need help!" Ali cried out, down the hall. "Help, please!" The fear and adrenaline going through her body made it easy for her to produce tears. "Oh God, please! She needs help!"

Finally, they could hear the sound of footsteps hurrying down the hall. To their pleasure and dismay, the deputy and DJ had both responded.

"What's wrong with her?" the deputy asked, looking through the bars at Christine.

"We don't know! One minute she was going to sleep and the next this happened," Ali explained, tears still flowing. "Please! She needs medical help!"

The deputy looked to DJ silently for permission to open the door. DJ nodded and stood next to him as he fumbled with the keys. "Oh my God, hurry, please hurry!" Ali cried out once more.

Caden and Zach were on either side of Christine, pretending to check her pulse and fan her down. Once the deputy was inside the cell, they pounced. Caden took the deputy down with a clothesline, while Zach focused on taking away his gun. DJ began to enter the cell, but Ali stopped him.

"We are getting out of here," she said, her voice strong and clear. Behind her, she heard grunting and punching, but she didn't take her eyes off DJ.

"I can't let you do that, Ali," DJ responded, slowly walking towards her, pushing her further into the cell. "I have to hand you guys over."

"Why are you doing this?" she asked, still focused on

his movements, trying to buy time for the guys to overtake the deputy.

"You and Caden are they key. They need you," DJ answered frankly.

Ali cocked her head to the side and took a quick glance at the fight that was now happening beside her. She caught a glimpse of Zach's bloody face. DJ took advantage of this distraction to dive for Ali. At the last second she moved to the side, out of his grasp, hitting her head on the top bunk. She stood dazed, trying to focus on DJ and the fight going on.

"Ali, there's nowhere to go," DJ pointed out, now leaning against the wall opposite her. "No one is going to just let you walk out the door."

Suddenly a gun shot rang out. The fight came to an abrupt stop and everyone turned their eyes in the direction of the sound. Christine stood in the open doorway, shotgun in hand. During the scuffle, no one had noticed Christine crawl out of the cell. She had closed the other cell doors, rightly trapping the ones that were after them.

"Christine, where…" Ali began.

"Ali, really? No questions, right now, okay?" She stood,

shotgun ready and pointed directly at DJ. Ali took a gulp of air into her lungs and nodded.

"Okay, this is how this is going to work." Christine's voice was steady without a hint of panic or hesitation. "We are going to leave and you two are going to stay here, in this cell."

Zach and Caden rose up from the floor, holding onto the deputy. Ali began to move towards Christine, ensuring that she did not block her clear shot. Out of the corner of her eye, she saw DJ move against the wall, making no attempts to stop her.

"You won't get far. Gemma and the others will be here to collect you in a few minutes," DJ said calmly, not concerned of the fact that a shotgun was pointed directly at this chest.

"We'll take our chances," Christine remarked sarcastically.

Ali now stood behind her friend, willing the guys to hurry.

"I got him, Zach," Caden offered, looking at his best friend and seeing his bloody nose and the purple and blue bruises beginning to form all over his pale face.

Once Zach had loosened his grip on the deputy, the deputy threw his head back, knocking him squarely in the chest. DJ made a move for Caden and another shot rang out in the air. The deputy fell in a slump to the ground, blood pooling underneath his body. The guys stood still, looking down at the body. When they looked up, they saw that Christine had fired the gun, again aiming at DJ's chest.

"Come on, guys."

Caden and Zach walked out of the cell, shutting the door behind them. Christine lowered the gun and her resolve began to crumble as she stared at the lifeless man.

"Come on, Chris." Ali gently pulled on her elbow.

Christine walked away with her friend, subtlety shaking.

"Where did you get the shotgun, Chris?" Caden gently asked her, not wanting to startle her.

It took a few seconds before she was able to respond. "From the main office, I smashed the cabinet glass."

Zach fell against the wall, and they all rushed to his side. "I'm okay, that last hit was tough." He slid down the wall, sitting on the floor to rest.

Ali and Caden left him and Christine alone to go to the

office. As they walked past the other cells, they could hear the others yelling at them, vowing to collect them and get vengeance. They entered the office and went to the gun cabinet, after grabbing two more shotguns and shells; they went back for Christine and Zach. Zach had his eyes closed and looked close to sleep.

"Zach, come on, Zach, we have to get moving," Ali urged, looking at Caden for help lifting him.

"Just five more minutes," he pleaded.

"Zach, we don't have five minutes, we need to move, now." Ali passed the shotgun over to Christine and grabbed one of his arms as Caden threw the strap over his shoulder and took the other. They lifted him onto his feet. When they got to the entrance, they saw Gemma approaching the station with her father, Bobby, and a few others. Ali muttered a curse under her breath, as they ducked behind a partition.

"What do we do now?" she asked.

They stayed low, as they heard the front door open. Christine cocked an eyebrow, clearly asking how she did that. Ali really wanted to throw her words from earlier back at her, but knew that now was not the time.

Holding their breath, they heard the others footsteps approaching, splitting around the partition to go to the cells on each side. Making themselves as small as possible and praying that the group wouldn't look around, they waited for their chance to escape. Once the last person had passed around the corner, they made a break for the door.

"Zach, you gotta run, baby," Christine said, as they lifted him up.

He barely nodded but tried to steady himself on his feet.

"Okay, on three." Caden took one last look around the corner, where a commotion was beginning. "Three!" he yelled.

They ran for the door, pushing on the entrance, finding it relocked.

"Oh no," Ali groaned in frustration.

They heard steps quickly approaching from behind them.

"Stand back, guys." Christine pumped the shotgun, then shot at the door.

Glass shattered and fell around them as they ran to the

SUV. Caden unlocked the door and put the keys into the ignition.

"It won't start!" he cried, trying desperately to turn the engine over.

Ali was bouncing in her seat as she saw Gemma, DJ and others running out of the station.

"We need to try a cruiser or something." Zach motioned to the car parked next to them.

"Ali, have you ever shot a gun?" Christine asked, as she handed Zach a pistol and Caden gave Ali back the shotgun.

"Are you serious? No!" Ali cringed as she felt the cold metal against her hand.

"Well, you're about to learn. Caden, we'll cover you as you try to start the cruiser, go!"

Caden looked at his little sister holding the shotgun and he was suddenly very scared. "Maybe I should," he began, reaching for the gun.

"Dude, we don't have time for this!" Christine nearly pulled Ali out of the front seat. "Go!"

Caden opened his door and ran to the closest cruiser, to find it locked. He began to run to the next car when one of Gemma's minions advanced on him.

"I got her," Zach shouted, running towards them, his second wind coming on.

Ali and Christine crouched next to the SUV, guns ready.

"When it's time to shoot, pump it once, that will place the shell in the chamber. Then pull the trigger, okay?" Christine told Ali in a rush.

Before Ali could reply, Christine stood and shot, aiming for anyone that came close. Ali took a deep breath and stood, ready to fire at the first thing that moved.

"Don't kill them, we must take them alive!" she heard Gemma yell from the steps of the station.

"What the hell is she talking about?" Christine asked, keeping an eye on Zach and Caden who had made it into a cruiser and were trying to start it up.

"I'm not sure, something about me and Caden are keys?" She shrugged. "I'll fill you in later, but right now we got to go!"

The crowd was now moving over to the cruiser, grabbing at the doors, trying to disable it. Christine and Ali ducked behind the SUV and began to move. As silently and quickly as they could, they snuck up on the cruiser; Ali raised her gun, sight fixed on Mr. Curtis' chest, finger on the trigger when she heard footsteps behind her. She whipped around, shotgun still raised and what she saw made her heart stop.

Gemma had DJ pushed down onto his hands and knees, head bowed down towards Ali.

"Ali, Ali, Ali," Gemma said in her sugary sweet voice, shaking her head, "you really thought you were going to make it, didn't you?"

Ali didn't respond as she stood there, looking her dead in the eye. Gemma smiled; kicking DJ in the back and watching as he sprawled on the ground in front of her.

"Now, you four come with me or," she looked down at DJ still lying on the ground, "I'll have to dispose of him."

Ali gawked at how causally Gemma said those last words. "You wouldn't?" she whispered.

Gemma gave out a tinkling laugh, and then her silvery blue eyes turned cold. Ali turned to Christine who had the shotgun pointed at Mr. Curtis; she flicked her eyes to Ali and gave her a slight shrug before returning to the threat in front of her.

"You have until I count to five," Gemma stated and she began to examine her nails. "One."

Ali looked down at DJ.

"Two."

DJ looked up at Ali, giving her a wink. Confused, she looked back at Gemma.

"Three."

Before Gemma could take her next breath, DJ pulled at her leg and Ali watched as Gemma shrieked and fell on her back. At the sound of Gemma's shriek, her father turned towards the sound, seeing his daughter, their leader in trouble, he motioned for a few of the others to advance on them.

Ali stood frozen in place, holding the shotgun steady. She turned at the sound of running footsteps and in one fluid motion, pulled the trigger and sent a shell into Mr. Curtis' chest. Christine was coming up quickly, carrying extra shells in one hand.

She quickly took in the situation, placing four shells into her gun. With a steady hand she took out the middle-age couple running towards them. Ali turned back to DJ and Gemma to see that they were still struggling on the parking lot.

DJ was trying to hold onto Gemma, but she was a strong fighter. She was able to match DJ's advances blow for blow, almost as if she could read his mind. As soon as he would get a grip on her, she would counter with some mind bending move to escape him.

The remaining others were coming out of the station quickly now, dividing up to try to surround them. Christine and Ali stood back to back, Christine defending Ali; Ali defending DJ.

In the background she could hear Caden calling to them, but his voice barely registered. The fight unfolding before her was getting harder and harder to watch. Gemma was clearly gaining the upper hand.

"I thought I trained you better, DJ," she sneered, again blocking the feeble punch that was thrown at her. "We spent years preparing for this!" she spat out, her anger showing through her carefully built façade. She began circling DJ in a way a lion might circle a wounded gazelle.

"And then you what? Went and fell in love? Trying to protect the only ones that weren't infected?" She sent a kick into his side and DJ balled up in pain. "We weren't designed for love!"

Ali was having a hard time following the conversation and defending herself. She could feel Christine struggling to do the same. They heard a car pull up behind him, with a glance Ali saw Caden fly out of the passenger side, holding a 9mm.

"Get in the car!" he ordered.

Both girls stood their ground, both needing to find out more, one wanting to rescue DJ. With a curse, Caden grabbed Christine's arm and began to pull her towards the car. Ali turned back to Gemma and DJ. DJ was curled up on the asphalt, blood trickling from his mouth and ear. He looked up at her and tried to give her a smile, but winced instead.

Ali raised her shotgun at Gemma's chest. "Step back, Gemma," she warned.

Gemma's cruel laughter sent chills down her spine. When Ali heard the 'pop pop' of the 9mm coming from a few feet besides her, she barely flinched, pumping the shotgun instead. Gemma kneeled next to DJ, clasping his head between her hands. Ali pulled the trigger, only to hear the hallow sound of an empty chamber. Gemma's lips curled into a smile that didn't reach her cold eyes. The last sound that Ali heard before Caden picked her up and carried her away was the sound of DJ's neck breaking.

⁂

"I could have saved him," Ali whispered; huddled into the corner of the backseat.

"Sis, it's not your fault," Caden tried to soothe her.

She just shook her head and looked out the window, letting the tears fall down her cheeks.

"Ali, no offense…" Zach began from behind the steering wheel, but Christine's cough cut him off.

"Ali, at least you knew that he really did love you," Christine said loudly enough to get the guy's attention.

Ali then began to recount the things that Gemma had said while they had been fighting. Once she was finished, Ali cried quietly into Christine's shoulder while Zach and Caden sat stunned.

"He was trying to help you escape?" Caden asked, not

believing what Christine had said.

"Yes, he was." Christine was patting at Ali's braids, whispering into her ear that things were going to be alright.

"What did Gemma mean they weren't designed to love?" Zach asked.

"Who knows what that crazy bitch meant," Christine muttered, giving him a stern look through the rearview mirror as the mention of Gemma's name sent Ali into a fresh wave of tears.

"And what does it mean that we aren't infected?"

"DJ said Caden and I are the key," Ali whispered with a hiccup.

"The key?" Christine's brow furrowed.

"Yeah, when we were trying to escape the cell, he said that they wouldn't let us go, because we are the key."

That prompted another round of discussion throughout the group, but Ali wanted to have nothing to do with it. She returned her gaze out the window and replayed her last few minutes with DJ. She was about to curse herself, yet again, for not checking her gun, when Zach slammed on the brakes.

The entrance to the freeway was blocked by cars.

"How did they do this?" Caden pondered, watching as Zach tried another entrance, only to find it blocked as well.

"Man, they even blocked the exits!"

"Well, when your leader is a psychopathic murderous bitch, I guess anything is possible," Ali piped up. And despite the seriousness of situation, she felt the pull of a smile tug her lips and heard the others laugh.

"You going to be okay, sis?" Caden asked, true concern plastered over his face.

"Eventually."

They cruised around town, looking for a route of escape only to find the major ways out of Tucson blocked, either by cars or other roadblocks that had been set up. They had also noticed the streets had become deserted, no one to be seen.

"Where do you think they are?" Christine asked, looking around the neighborhood they had cut through to try another path.

"I have no idea," Zach said, "but we are going to need to switch out vehicles and find a place to hole up until we can figure something out."

They drove to another neighborhood and looked for signs of life. Again, nothing caught their attention.

"Let's find something here," Ali suggested. "They are probably waiting for us to show back up at one of our houses anyway."

Zach pulled the cruiser in an alleyway.

"What are you doing, dude?" Caden asked.

"We don't want to leave it in plain sight, do we?" Zach slowly drove down the alley until he found a backyard with a gate.

"Wait here, we're going to check things out," he told the girls, both of whom began to protest, only to realize that they had no way of getting out anyway.

Caden and Zach hopped the fence to check out the house and make sure it was safe.

"Ugh, Zach probably loves the fact that for once, I have to listen to him." Christine crinkled her nose and winked at Ali. She scooted over to her friend and pulled her into an awkward hug. "You miss him, don't you?"

Ali nodded her head and tears slowly began to fall down her cheeks.

"How could I think he was going to hurt us, Chris?" she whispered. "He never tried to hurt me, so why did I think he would do it now?"

Christine remained silent, not wanting to point out that he did lock them in a jail cell and he was going to turn them over to Gemma, but she knew that it was easier for her to remember him as she chose to right now. The tap at the window startled both girls; Ali fumbled with the shotgun, realizing that she had no room to maneuver.

"Hold on, Pistol Annie." Caden threw his hands up in mock surrender. "It's safe; we'll be opening the gate and letting you out."

Ali's heart was racing as she watched Zach pull open the gate and Caden drive the cruiser into the backyard. Caden feigned losing the keys as Christine threw curse words at him in both English and Spanish from the backseat. Once the girls were out of the cruiser, they all walked into the house together.

"Wait!" Ali hissed, as Caden reached for the light switch, "let's wait and see if anyone else turns the lights on or if anyone returns, before we alert everyone that we're here!"

Caden stuck his tongue out at his sister, but withdrew his hand from the switch.

They began to swiftly move about the home, looking for items they could carry with them, but coming up surprisingly empty.

"Do these people not eat?" Zach grunted, as he closed yet another cabinet.

"Calm down, sweetheart, we'll find something." Christine opened and shut the refrigerator door quickly, not wanting Zach to see that it was empty also.

Ali and Caden also weren't having much luck checking out the garage for supplies.

"No light bulbs, no cans of bug spray," Ali stated, thinking of their own cluttered garage. "Not even a speck of oil on the ground."

"Either these people just moved in and hadn't gone shopping yet, or they knew this was coming." Caden huffed out, finally gave up and returned inside the house, Ali following after a few moments.

She ducked her head into an open door and saw that it was a small powder room.

"Hey, there's a restroom back here, no windows! I'm going to freshen up," she called down the hall.

Ali turned on the light and closed the door behind her, staring at the person reflected back at her in the mirror. She seemed to look the same; caramel skin, black braids, grey-blue eyes, yet somehow different. The softness that was there earlier was now gone, as was the spark that was just beneath the surface of her eyes.

She somehow looked... older.

With a sigh, she turned the tap on and cupped her hands to fetch water. When the water began to flow, she remembered just in time to pull them back, but not quick enough. A few drops touched her skin, and a scream flew from her lips.

CHAPTER TEN

"Ali!" Christine yelled, running down the hall to the bath. "Ali!" She tried the knob, banging on the door. "Ali, let me in!"

Caden and Zach were pushing Christine out of the way ready to break the door down when they heard her unlock it.

Slowly pushing the door open, they saw Ali leaning against the basin, slowly breathing in and out, her skin cold and clammy with sweat.

"Ali, sweetie, what happened?" Christine asked, quickly looking over her, not seeing any visible signs of injury.

"The water…" Ali began, cut off by the shaking that was taking over her body.

"The water?" Christine glanced at the sink, the brown sludge still flowing down from the open tap. "What about the water?"

With a shaky hand, Ali reached for the water again with her index finger, a shower of sparks erupted where the water touched her skin. The others let out shouts of surprise and then confusion as the sparks continued.

"How are you doing that?" Caden demanded, nudging Christine out of the way.

"I don't know," she said. "But I'm sure you guys can do it too." She took her finger away from the sink, drying it on her jeans. "I mean, if what DJ said was true."

Christine and Zach gave each other curious looks before she stepped forward and repeated Ali's actions. Just as Ali had predicted, once the water touched Christine's skin sparks began to fly.

"That is wicked." Christine smiled, playing with the water and the sparks that shot off of her hand.

"Okay, that's enough," Zach said, as he pulled her hand back, careful not to touch the water himself. "How do you know that stuff isn't going to hurt you?"

Ali gave them a grim look as she turned the water off. "Because we've already been drinking it."

Caden's head snapped up. "No, we haven't!" he instantly protested.

"Yes, we have." Zach nodded in agreement, rubbing his head as if a headache was coming on.

"When?" he demanded.

"The coffee," Christine and Ali said in unison.

"We've been drinking coffee since the quake happened," Christine answered, thinking back about the pot they shared at the Morgan house and the cups the deputy gave them.

"So for, what, the past three days?"

"Yeah, at least," Ali answered her. "And if it was going to hurt us, or turn us into Gemma's mind controlled groupies, it would have kicked in by now, I think." She heard Caden give a sigh and shouldered her way out of the bathroom.

They followed her down the hallway to the living room. They all eyed the couch with envy and dread. After a few moments of silence, Christine began to giggle, giddiness taking over her body.

"Why don't we see how many bedrooms there are," she began, "then if there are enough, we won't have to kill each other for the couch."

The lack of sleep was apparent after that statement, as none of them had even considered it before. They walked around the house and found that it did have enough rooms for all of them, but no one was particularly keen on sleeping alone.

"Why don't you girls go ahead and get some sleep?" Zach suggested. "Caden and I will keep first watch, and then you two can take over when you get up."

"Yeah, I figure Pistol Annie over there won't shoot one of us on accident," Caden kidded, nudging Ali with his elbow.

"Keep it up and I'll claim that I shot you on accident," she teased back, giving him a playful squeeze, grateful that he was still with her.

Christine gave Zach a kiss and hugged Caden, while Ali said goodnight to them both, with a small wave the girls walked to the master bedroom.

"You asleep?" Christine asked after several minutes of silence had passed.

"Nope."

"You close to be being asleep?" Christine probed further.

"Chris, what do you have on your mind?" Ali propped herself up on her elbow and looked at her friend with exasperation written all over her face.

"Don't look at me like that!" Christine said, sticking her tongue out at her.

"Well, what's up? I know you have something going on in that pretty head of yours."

"I've just been thinking about what DJ said, about you being the key?"

Ali just nodded her head.

"Well, could the *four* of us be keys? And if so, how could we be the only four in Tucson not to be infected by the quake and that weird sludge?"

Christine saw the moment Ali had an idea.

"Wait, we aren't." Ali sat up.

"What?"

"Remember what Michelle said? That they killed Mr. McCobo because he wouldn't conform?" Ali saw a sadness pass over Christine's eyes.

"My mom said the same thing about Nando."

"Oh, my God, I am so sorry Chris." Ali put her arms around her.

"It's okay," Christine said, brushing her tears away. "What were you saying?"

Ali took a deep breath, her mom flashing through her mind. "What if they killed everyone that didn't change?"

"Gemma did say not to kill us when we were escaping," Christine remembered.

"That's right, so we must not be infected, I mean we've all been exposed and none of us have tried to kill each other, so I'm guessing it's a good bet that we're all okay."

Ali wrinkled her nose and laid her head back on the pillow. She couldn't lie; she had been wondering the same thing.

"It just doesn't make sense, why us?" She continued to stare at the ceiling, dismissing each crazy thought that came into her head.

"You know what we have to do, don't you?" Christine continued to urge. "Don't you?"

With a sigh, Ali sat up and looked Christine in eye. "Yes, I know."

"But the guys aren't going to like it."

A few hours later, they emerged from the bedroom and switched off with Zach and Caden, who opted not to share the bed.

The girls sat quietly, waiting for them to fall asleep before they began the first part of their plan. A half hour passed before they heard the rhythmic snoring of the guys.

"Are you sure you want to do this?" Ali asked one last time, as they tiptoed to the kitchen.

"Yes, we have to," Christine replied, determined to get to the bottom of things.

"Okay," Ali sighed out.

They entered the kitchen and turned the faucet on, watching the brown sludge come out in a thick column.

"Together?" Christine asked, her voice faltering for the first time.

"Together." Ali smiled encouragingly. They cupped their hands and placed them under the stream, ignoring the sparks that flew from them. Taking a couple gulps of the water, the girls turned off the faucet and returned to the living room, each now armed with their shotguns.

"Okay. Straight from the source water," Ali stated, as she plopped down on the living room floor.

"Yep, nothing hiding it," Christine replied, as she sat, facing Ali.

"You know I won't be able to kill you, right?" Ali asked her, realizing now that they were face-to-face with what a horrible idea this was.

"Me neither, but let's hope we're right and we don't have to."

They sat there watching each other, flinching at every twitch or sudden movement the other made. Finally, after a couple of hours, they began to relax.

"It's been a while; I think it would have happened by now," Christine offered, placing her shotgun down, but still within reach.

"I think so too," Ali agreed, but also keeping the shotgun handy. The sun was beginning to set and neither girl wanted to be alone with the other, but they didn't know how to say it.

"Oh this is ridiculous!" Ali stood up, throwing her hands up in frustration. "I know you're not going to turn and you know I'm not going to turn, so let's just stop this!" She towered over Christine and waited for her to answer, her chest heaving in and out.

Christine wouldn't meet her gaze at first, but slowly raising her head to look at her friend, she shook her head. "You're crazy, you know that?"

They let out tension breaking laughter and fell back into easy conversation after that, sitting back to back, so they could keep an eye on both entrances. They had forgotten to ask the guys if they had seen anyone walking around during their shift, but even now, not one person had passed by the front window.

As darkness crept into the room, a new uneasiness began to fall upon them and they held the guns a little closer and began to speak in whispers.

Ali wanted to move closer to the front window and peek out, to see if anyone had begun to move around to look for them, but Christine was against the idea.

"What if they see you?" she whispered.

"Then I could see them too and we would have a lot more warning to get the hell out of here."

Ali was about to chide Christine for her behavior, but remembered that Christine had always been afraid of the dark. She felt foolish for letting this slip her mind, and instead of arguing about the window, she rested her head against her friend's legs. She felt Christine's rigid body begin to relax.

"I'm sorry, Chris, I forgot," Ali whispered.

"It's okay, there's been a lot going on lately."

Ali could feel drops falling, her forehead getting wet and realized that Christine was crying.

"What's wrong, baby?" Ali asked, realizing that was probably the stupidest question she could have come up with.

"She killed him, Ali. Our own mother killed Nando."

Ali nodded her head, unsure of whether Christine could see her or not, pushing back her own emotions.

"I'm sorry, Chris, so very sorry." Ali sat there and let Christine continue to cry on her shoulder.

A few minutes later, they heard the bedroom door open and then close again. One set of footsteps were slowly entering the room.

"You guys in here?" It was Caden.

"We're over here," Ali whispered, guiding her brother to them.

"Why didn't you wake us up before the sun went down?" Caden scolded. "You know we don't want you guys to deal with them alone."

"Calm down, C, we haven't seen hide nor hair of anyone since you guys went to sleep," Ali explained, still soothing Christine and thankful the darkness hid her tears. "Plus, it's not like Zach is getting up... any... time..." she trailed off.

"Ali, what's wrong?" Christine whispered, quickly picking up on Ali's tension.

"Someone's out there," she whispered.

Christine and Caden quickly turned around to face the window, and saw a figure outlined by the street lights. Christine lifted the shotgun, ready to pump it, when Caden placed a hand on her knee.

In the darkness, she could barely see him shaking his head 'no.' They heard him cock the nine as quietly as he could, leaning in close to Christine, he whispered for her to go get Zach.

Ali felt movement to her right and felt Caden slide next to her.

"Don't move, sis," he whispered, eyes locked on the figure still standing at the window.

Her eyes were glued to the same spot, wondering how many more were outside, if they were surrounding the house, would they be able to escape?

"Hey," Christine whispered.

Ali let out a small shriek before covering her mouth with her hands. Taking in deep breathes; Ali wrapped her hands around the shotgun, wishing Christine could see the look that was currently on her face.

"Ssh!" Caden harshly whispered, quietly moving to the front of the house.

She could see her brother's outline next to the window, gun raised and ready. Taking quick glances out of the window, she heard him mutter a curse and saw his outline disappear again.

"Okay, there are three of them out there, just standing in the yard. They might be looking at the house or sleeping for all I can tell," Caden explained.

"Shit," Zach muttered, "what about the backyard?"

Ali suddenly realized that she hadn't thought about the backyard and felt the goose bumps return to her arms. She heard the boys tiptoe to the backdoor and return quickly.

"Clear," Zach whispered, as he crouched next to Christine.

"So, now what?" Christine asked, eyes still glued to the front window, "make a run for it in the cruiser?"

"Do we really have another option?" Caden whispered back.

As quickly and quietly as they could they gathered their things and walked out the backdoor on alert, not sure if they were truly alone in the yard.

Walking to the cruiser, Ali's senses were on high alert, she held the shotgun close, ready to pump and fire at a moment's notice. Every cricket chirp, every pick up of the breeze made her heart race. Christine followed closely behind her, covering her back.

Standing beside the cruiser, the boys followed, Zach slipping behind the wheel; Caden moving towards the gate.

Taking a deep breath and sending up a prayer, Caden pulled the gate open and checked the alleyway.

Standing at one end of the alley were four more people. Again, not moving, just staring. Caden motioned for Ali and Christine to get in the car and for Zach to pull out.

"Let's get out of here," Caden said, keeping an eye on the small group staring at them.

"Thataway?" Zach joked, hooking a thumb in the opposite direction.

Caden just nodded as the cruiser moved forward.

As they rounded the corner to approach the main street, Ali turned around and saw that the three people from the front of the house had now joined the others watching the house, standing there frozen in place.

As the car disappeared into the darkness, one smiled and spoke aloud, "Yes, mistress, they have left."

⚜

"How did they find us?" Zach wondered out loud. "We didn't do anything to attract attention!"

The girls gave each other a look, "Well, we might

have," Christine said, getting the guys' full attention.

"What did you do?" Zach demanded.

"Yeah, what? Go outside and yell 'Over here! Over here!?'" Caden accused.

"No, we didn't do that," Ali snapped at him. "We… well… we did an experiment," she said in a much quieter tone.

Zach stopped the car and turned to face them. "You did an experiment? What kind of experiment?"

Taking a deep breath, Ali explained that they had decided to drink the water while the boys were asleep, and how they had sat armed and were ready to fire at each other if one of them had indeed turned.

"You did what?!" Zach yelled at Christine. "How could you do that without telling me?" Zach threw open the cruiser's door and then opened Christine's, pulling her out into the night. "Did you think, for one second, what that could have done to me?" he yelled at her.

"Zach, I…" Christine began, voice raised to match his.

"Don't you dare!" Zach told her, his voice now steely and cold. "Don't you dare try to rationalize this. Don't you get how much I love you?" Before Christine could defend herself any further, Zach pulled her in and kissed her.

Christine began to pull away, but Zach's grasp was iron tight.

Ali and Caden turned away, shocked by Zach's angry outburst, but also embarrassed by the display of affection that was now happening a few feet away from them.

"If clothing starts to come off, please turn on the siren," Ali said. When Caden didn't answer, she knew that she was in trouble. "C…"

"Don't 'C' me. Ali, how could you guys do something like that without telling us? What if it had failed? What if Christine had to kill you?"

Caden turned to face her, his face contorted in unshed tears. "What if you died, like Mom? What would happen to me?"

Ali was speechless.

The thought of leaving Caden alone hadn't crossed her mind once. She now realized how selfish their experiment had been and now she had another reason to be thankful that it had failed. Or had it just had a different result?

"Caden, I am so sorry." She began to reach for him, but stopped, remembering that she was in the back of a police car. "We really need to switch out cars."

Caden let out a small snort, but got out of the car and let her out.

She wrapped her arms around her brothers waist, thanking her mom or God or whoever was watching over them and keeping them together.

"I am truly sorry, Caden, I didn't think it was going to work, but we should have told you guys what we were up to." She hadn't noticed that she had tilted her head to the left side, much like how her mother used to do when she was deep in thought.

"Sis, what's up?" Caden asked her, recognizing the stance.

"You know how Christine said we might have attracted the attention?"

Caden nodded his head, confused.

"Well, what if it's the water?" Ali's eyes began to sparkle. "What if that's how they found us?" She was about to explain further when they heard Christine and

Zach approaching.

"You two okay?" Ali asked her best friend, even though the two were holding hands and Christine was leaning into Zach's side.

"Yeah, we're okay... you two?" Christine asked.

Caden and Ali smiled, and he nudged her with his elbow.

"Yeah, short stuff here begged me for forgiveness and told me that I was the best brother on earth." He gave them a wink. "How could I not forgive her?"

Ali sighed, but smiled, just happy that everything was forgiven.

"So what were you guys talking about?" Zach asked, holding tightly onto Christine.

"I'm just trying to put everything together," she said, giving him a meaningful look.

"Yeah, but I don't think we're going to be able to do that."

Ali gave Christine a look, her eyes starting to sparkle again. "I think I have a piece figured out."

"You don't mean…" Christine trailed off, a smile spreading across her face.

"Yep," Ali answered her.

"Oh my God, why didn't we think of that before!" Christine was nearly bouncing with excitement.

"Do you have any idea, at all, what they're talking about?" Zach asked Caden.

"Actually, yeah, I kinda do."

"When Christine and I drank the water, we had to turn the faucet on right?" Ali started to explain.

"Well, yeah." Zach shrugged, still not following.

"What if that's how they tracked us? I mean, from what we've been able to tell, we are the only ones left *not* affected by the water," Ali explained, hoping that she was being clear.

"By turning on the water tap?" Zach asked, before Christine let out a sigh.

"Yes," she said, clearly exasperated. "Because why else would anyone else turn one on?"

The light began to shine behind Zach's blue eyes as

understanding dawned on him. "Ah, okay."

Ali and Christine exchanged another look; one that they knew was not going to go over well.

"Okay, so here's the plan…" Ali began, realizing that she was the only one that could call this shot. "We find another car, now," she added, looking at Caden's smug face. "And then we go get answers."

"Okay, the car should be easy, but answers?" Zach asked. "I don't see how we're going to be able to do that."

"You're right, we're not." Ali led the group back to the cruiser, then turned and faced everyone. "Not without help." She leaned against the cruiser and braced herself.

"We need to find Gemma."

CHAPTER ELEVEN

Caden and Zach continued their argument with Ali as they set out to find a new vehicle.

"Sis, this is suicidal!" he tried once more. "She wants us! Shouldn't we be trying to get the hell out Dodge instead of handing ourselves over?"

Frustrated with the duel attack, Ali spun around to face him. "And go where? Do what?" Ali scowled and threw her hands up. "I have a feeling that this isn't only happening here in Tucson. So where can we go?"

When his face went blank, she knew that he hadn't thought that far ahead.

"They've blocked all of our escape routes; I doubt we could make it very far without water or transportation." She turned to look at everyone. "Seriously, what are we supposed to do? She is not going to leave us alone." She wanted that last part to sink in.

She knew she was right, and she needed them to know it as well. There was no way they were going to run from this.

"If we are the only ones not infected, then yes, that

means that Gemma wants us and she wants us bad." She took a deep breath before she laid the final blow. "And I'm going to make sure she gets us."

Her statement was met with silence, as she had expected and she braced herself for the backlash. When silence continued to drag on, she began to walk forward again, this time towards a black sedan parked in front of an apartment complex.

"Ali," she heard Zach call to her a few yards away, she continued walking towards the car; determined not to let them talk her out of her plan.

"Ali!" Zach yelled at her again, this time running to catch up. He grabbed her arm and pulled her to face him.

"What the hell are you talking about? You're going to hand us over to her?"

The anger in his voice made her flinch, but she shook it off and stood her ground.

"Yeah, I am." She tried to break his hold by pulling her arm, but his grip was too tight.

"You're crazy!" he screamed, spit flying from his mouth.

QUAKE

Ali had never seen Zach so angry, his outburst from earlier seemed mild compared to this.

Christine was doing her best to hold Caden back, letting them work things out.

"Let me go, Zach," she told him in a calm, cool voice. "I have a plan, and I need my arm to be able to shoot that bitch if it goes right."

Zach was shocked by the calmness of Ali's voice and let her go.

"What do you mean you're going to shoot her?" Caden asked, coming to stand beside them, glaring at his best friend for being so rough with his sister.

Ali rubbed her arm where Zach had held it tightly, moving closer to her brother. She was still working on the plan herself, but she had played her hand early, so she had no other choice but to tell them so.

"I'm still working this out as we go, but this is what I've thought out so far." She looked around the small circle they made up.

"First off, we need to find a new mode of transportation. They've spotted us in the cruiser and will be looking out for it."

Everyone nodded in agreement.

"Second, we need to find more guns," she couldn't believe she was the one suggesting this, "smaller ones, something that can be hidden." With everyone taking in that piece of news she continued on, "Once we've done that, we need to return to our house."

Caden caught the small catch in her voice when she spoke of their home.

"That is the one place they are sure to be keeping an eye on. That's where we let them take us." She paused to see if they were still with her.

"And then?" Zach demanded.

"I have no idea; I was hoping someone would help out with that part."

No one looked at her as one or the other was shuffling their feet or looking towards the sky, thinking. Christine had her arms wrapped around herself, staring off into space. Ali let out a sigh and began to walk towards the sedan again.

It was parked in a slot marked 17D, looking at the

apartment building she figured out which section the apartment should be located in and began to walk away.

"Ali, where are you going?" Caden called after her.

"To get some keys."

She silently walked into the dark walkway, listening intently for signs of anyone else being there. Looking at the windows that lined her path, no light shone, not even the soft bluish glow of a television.

Ali quickly determined that apartment 17D would be on the second floor of the building and swiftly climbed the stairs. Tiptoeing her way to the apartment, she became aware that she wasn't alone.

Pressing herself against the building, she held her breath as someone moved on the path in front of her. Wishing she had brought someone with her or at least the nine millimeter, her mind began to race with ideas she could use to protect herself, nothing came to mind.

Cursing herself for never taking a self-defense class, she waited. The person was just a few feet away, walking slowly, as if they were just out for a midnight stroll.

Ali risked moving her head just a fraction of an inch to the right to see if she could make out who the person was. When their face came into view, she let out a small gasp before she could stop herself.

Once the person heard the noise, she stopped and a slow smile crept across her face.

Stepping closer to Ali was Christine's mom.

�֎

"I must collect you," she said, reaching her hand out to Ali.

Ali began to back away, wondering if she would be able to outrun her and if any others were with her.

"It's no use," Ms. Lopez spoke to her. "We will find you wherever you go." Ali froze. Gemma was projecting through her.

"What? What do you mean?"

Christine's mom said nothing, she just continued to walk towards her, hand still extended.

"We must collect you," she whispered now inches from Ali.

Feeling the woman's hot breath woke Ali up and she began to move again. Looking around, she saw a broom leaning against the wall and reached for it. Using all the strength she could, she swung the broom at the woman's head.

The other woman groaned at the contact, but continued to try to grab Ali. Ali swung again, this time aiming for the midsection. Ms. Lopez grabbed at the broom and yanked it out of Ali's grasp, making her stumble on her own feet and fall.

"We must collect you."

Ali used her hands to help back herself away from the woman in front of her.

"Please, Ms. Lopez, you don't want to do this," she whispered.

Just then she heard footsteps running into the walkway.

"Ali!" Christine called out.

"Here!" Ali screamed back, twisting her head around to look for another weapon.

She heard two sets of footsteps coming up the stairs before the shotgun blast rang out. She watched as Ms.

Lopez crumpled into a heap before her. Caden's hands clasped her arms and helped her up as Christine stood at the top of the stairs, shotgun still raised. She was taking several deep breaths with her eyes closed.

Ali fell into Caden's embrace, shaking as tears streamed down her face. Christine came beside them and laid a hand on Ali's shoulder.

"Ali, are you okay?"

Ali kept her eyes shut, as she pulled away from them, walking straight to the railing before she threw up.

⁂

Ali and Christine sat on a couch in apartment 17D once Caden placed a well-aimed kick at the door. While searching the kitchen, Zach found soda in the fridge and passed them around, before shuffling to a corner with his hands in his pockets, not sure what else he could do.

Ali leaned against the back, totally exhausted and embarrassed.

"Are you okay, sis?" Caden asked for the third time, worried about this reaction to her latest run-in.

"She just appeared," she whispered. "She knew that we

were going to be here." Remembering what Ms. Lopez had said.

"She knew?" Zach asked her.

"Yeah, she said that 'it doesn't matter,' they will always know where we are…" she broke off, remembering the most chilling detail.

"And… for a second," she still wasn't sure if it was true or just the fear, "for a second, it sounded like Gemma was talking through her."

"How?" Caden asked.

Ali just shook her head and closed her eyes. She just wanted to sleep. "I don't know. I truly, just, don't know."

Christine suddenly jumped up. "Come on, we have to go get the guns."

Zach tried to pull her back to him, but she shook his hand off.

"If they can find us 'wherever' we go, if Gemma can project herself through them, we need to protect ourselves. Let's go get the guns."

Ali opened her eyes and looked at Christine. She had

been peculiarly quiet after the shooting, shrugging off any form of contact.

"Chris, why don't we get some rest? We have enough ammo for the rest of the night and then we can start fresh in the morning," Caden replied, also picking up on her attitude change.

"I don't want to sleep! I want to go and find Gemma and hurt her as much as she's hurt us!" Christine shouted at them, her beautiful face scrunched up in anger. "I want to punch that two-faced bitch right in her face, and then shoot her sadistic brains out."

No one spoke or moved, too stunned by her outburst to intervene. She paced the small room, shotgun clutched tightly in her grasp. Ali knew that she should be feeling something, anything, but the extreme nothingness going through her body. *This isn't Christine.*

She glanced over to Zach who was still standing in the corner, with his hands balled up into fists. Caden finally stood and blocked Christine's path.

"You need to sleep." He held his hand up to silence her. "You do too, sis. Did you guys sleep at all the other night?"

Ali nodded her head, then remembering that they hadn't it, shook it.

She was so tired.

She was tired of thinking, tired of running, tired of trying to hold it together. Hadn't they just been arguing about turning themselves in? Why was that such a bad idea?

"Caden, I am so tired and so confused."

"Let's find you a bed." He led her down the short hallway to the single bedroom. As if she was a small child, he guided her to the small bed that was tucked into the corner.

"Lie down and sleep," he commanded.

She hugged him and nodded weakly, laying her head on the pillow and was fast asleep before he made it back to the door.

Once he returned to the living room, he saw that Christine was laying on the couch, fast asleep with Zach sitting sentinel on the floor by her head, the shotgun well in his reach.

"Is Ali out, too?" Zach asked, when Caden came and

sat next to him on the floor.

"Yeah, she was gone before her head hit the pillow." Caden noticed that Zach had switched off the overhead lights and had one small lamp on.

"Dude, what are we going to do?" Zach asked Caden, not taking his eyes off Christine. "Are we really going to go turn ourselves over to them, while somehow sneaking in a small arsenal? What in the hell is your sister thinking?"

Caden held up his hand, a warning. "Look, I'm not sure what Ali is thinking and I'm sure that once she gets some sleep, she'll see that her plan makes no sense," he looked right into Zach's eyes to make sure he was paying attention, "but if you ever lay a hand on my sister like that again? Gemma will be the least of your problems. Got it?"

Zach rolled his neck and looked over at Caden. "Man, I'm sorry, it's just..." he trailed off, looking at Christine's sleeping face.

"I know, man." Caden patted him on the shoulder. "I know. You love her. And I love my sister, so let's keep our heads straight and keep them safe. Deal?" Caden extended his hand to his best friend.

"I need you, man."

Zach looked at the outreached hand, debating whether to accept it or not. "I'm with you." Zach grabbed Caden's hand. "You take a shift and then I'll take a shift. Let's let the girls sleep all night."

Caden handed Zach the remaining shotgun shells then checked his gun and made sure the magazine was full. Realizing how depleted their store truly was, he knew that they were going to have to make a break for a gun store sooner rather than later. *But if Gemma and her lackeys truly knew where we're going to go, would it be worth it?*

"Alright man, I'm just going to do a quick sweep and see if there are any weapons here," he announced, shaking the thought off.

After rummaging through the apartment, the best Caden could come up with as weaponry was a flashlight and a brand new Rachel Ray skillet.

In a small cabinet next to the door, he found another pillow and blanket, which he threw at Zach and motioned for him to sleep. Zach looked at him with a mixture of gratitude and weariness.

Returning to the bedroom to check on Ali one last time, he flicked off the lamp and sat guard by the front door, nervous energy buzzing through his veins.

Every now and then his body tensed, convinced that he could hear people moving just outside the door, but he never checked, and if anyone was out there… they never bothered them. For now they were safe. Tomorrow was another day.

꧁꧂

Ali gazed out the car window, as they drove through the quiet streets. Waking up in a stranger's room had been disorienting and frightening, but once she calmed down and remembered where they were, she was thankful for the full night's sleep.

Walking into the living room, the sight had made her smile: Christine was asleep on the couch, with Zach on the floor beside her. Caden was sleeping against the loveseat being used as a barricade, and holding onto a skillet. She could only assume that they were supposed to switch off with their guard duty but they both fell asleep.

Now, after a quick breakfast of scrambled eggs and dry toast, they sat (as Caden so nicely put it) in a "borrowed" car, Zach driving them to the gun store. Tensions were still running high from the previous night with no one really knowing how to end it.

As Zach shifted gears, Ali cracked, "I really should have learned to drive a stick," hoping that Christine or one of the guys would laugh at the innuendo.

Caden did let out a snort, but no one else made a sound.

Glancing over at Christine, she looked deep in thought and Ali noticed that she had taken up the habit of tucking her hair behind her ears.

Ali reached over and gently tapped Christine on the shoulder, which seemed to snap her out of her daze.

"You okay?" Ali asked her gently.

Christine gave her a weak smile and nodded her head. "I really am sorry for losing it last night; I guess I just really needed some sleep."

A strain of hair fell into her face and Ali watched as she tucked it behind her ear before returning to look out the window again. Ali was about to try to reengage her in conversation, then thought better of it. Something was off about Christine and she just couldn't put her finger on it.

"So, um, does anyone know how to break into a heavily

secured gun store?" Zach asked, his voice heavy with sarcasm.

Ali glanced up and looked at him through the rearview mirror. It had never occurred to her that the place might be locked up tight.

"Uh…" she started, her gaze darting over to Caden who merely shrugged.

"That's what I thought," he muttered.

They continued to drive on for another twenty minutes or so before Zach pulled into the parking lot. The Armory was a Tucson mainstay, a deceptively plain gray building with no signage indicating its purpose.

Growing up, Ali had imagined that the building was truly a fortress, built during medieval times by a handsome prince to protect fairy princesses and their treasures from dragons. Her mom would laugh and laugh, asking her where she got such wild ideas.

"Well, there she is," Caden let out with a slow whistling following.

They climbed out of the car, glancing around to ensure that they hadn't been followed, or worse; somebody was waiting for them.

Approaching the store, Ali couldn't shake the feeling that they were 'casing the joint' as Caden and Zach peeked through windows and Christine tried the door.

"Well, they were able to lock up before they left."

"Hey! Come here!" Zach suddenly called out, motioning for everyone to come to the front window.

As they gathered around, Ali was able to see that the plate of glass wasn't protected by bars or any type of security grate. Peering into the store she saw several display cases and walls lined with weapons.

"So, do we just smash the glass and go in?" Christine asked, shading her eyes from the glare.

"That seems to be the best option, but what about an alarm?" Ali asked back, looking at a devious thin gold wire snaking its way across the top of the frame and towards the door.

"Well I don't think anyone is going to come arrest us." Caden smirked.

Ali rolled her eyes at him. "I'm not worried about the police; I'm worried about the noise." She stated, but began to look for something to smash the glass with.

Something else was bothering her, but before she could place a finger on it she heard Zach say; "Here, watch out," as he walked over to the car and popped the trunk.

Pulling out a crowbar, he walked back to the window and taking a baseball stance, swung with all his might at the window. The girls let out tiny yelps as the glass exploded around them.

"Well that solves that problem," Caden said, giving Zach an appreciative slap on the shoulder.

They entered the store, wary of the silence that welcomed them.

"I wonder why the alarm didn't go off," Ali whispered, afraid that if she spoke too loudly the alarm would begin to blare.

The sound of the glass crunching underneath their feet was unnerving enough as it was.

"Well, we're in, what do you want?" Zach asked, his face lighting up like a kid's on Christmas, the tension of the past evening finally evaporating.

Despite everything that they had been through the past

few days, Ali wasn't a fan of weaponry, but being surrounded by it now she had a newfound respect. Walking over to the display case that contained different types of pistols and revolvers, she ran her hand over the smooth glass, marveling at the array of guns.

Seeing a small, black gun in one of the display cases, she stopped.

"See something you like?" Christine asked, coming up behind her.

A bit surprised, Ali nodded. Christine walked up to the display case and using the butt of the shotgun smashed the glass. Gingerly, Ali picked up the small .45 out of the broken glass. After only using a shotgun, she was pleasantly surprised by its lightness and how easily it fit into her hand.

"Here, sis, it isn't going to work without these," Caden teased, tossing her a magazine.

She fumbled with it for a few minutes, swearing loudly until she heard it click into place. Looking up she saw Zach quietly laughing at her, as he tested out the scope on an assault rifle.

"How does the safety work?" she asked no one in

particular, studying the gun, realizing that the only time she really saw what a safety looked like was on television.

"Let me see," Caden said, taking the piece away from her. "Hmmm, looks like all you have to do is grip the stock to release the safety on this one."

Ali's face was a mixture of confusion and awe. Chuckling, Caden demonstrated what he meant then handed the gun back to her.

Placing the gun in the small of her back, it felt weird and foreign to her, though slowly the cold metal began to warm up against her skin and feel more comfortable.

Caden had taken a duffle bag off the shelf for the ammo and was debating between two Smith & Wesson handguns, while Zach was now playing with a crossbow. Ali was about to reach for another gun when she realized what had been nagging at her.

It was easy.

It was *too* easy! There should have been more protection guarding the store. If the owners had time to lock the front door, shouldn't they have had time to roll down the protective screens? Set an alarm? She turned to share her concerns with Caden when she realized that

Christine wasn't in the store.

"Guys, where's Chris?" She turned around in a circle quickly scanning the area.

Caden shrugged, while Zach jogged back to the restrooms to check.

Coming back, he shook his head and began to run to the front of the window.

CHAPTER TWELVE

Ali's heart plummeted to her stomach.

"Zach, wait!" It was too late, before she could finish the words; he was already out of the store. Caden began to follow him but Ali caught his arm.

"Ali, what's wrong?" Concern etched over his face.

"It was too easy." She shook her head, chiding herself for not realizing it before.

"*What* was too easy?" Frustration laced every word coming out of Caden's mouth; he was on the verge of saying something when they heard it, a small giggle.

It was her.

"Come out… come out wherever you are."

They both froze in their places, the childish taunt sending chills up and down their spines.

"I have Christine and Zach," she informed them, sounding almost bored. "Oh, and there is a gun to Zach's head. I suggest you don't make me ask again."

Ali began to walk towards the window, then paused. Checking to make sure the gun was still tucked into her jeans; she motioned for Caden to do the same.

"Are you crazy? You know she's going to search us!" he whispered harshly.

"Trust me," she told him, as she shoved a gun into his hands. Picking up a shotgun she moved to the front of the store.

Prepared to see Gemma's platoon of mindless followers, confusion quickly set in when they found that no one was waiting for them. The parking lot was eerily quiet.

"Come down the alley," Gemma demanded, still hidden from view.

Ali took Caden's hand and let him lead her around the building.

Coming around the corner, Ali let out a cry, her footsteps faltering. Instead of seeing Gemma, standing in front of dumpster was Christine, holding the shotgun to Zach's head.

"Oh my God, Christine, what are you doing?" Ali gasped.

"It is time to collect you," Christine stated.

"What?" Ali whispered, the familiar taunt making her weak in the knees.

"It is time to collect you," she repeated.

Zach was kneeling on the ground in front of her, a slight tremble going through his body.

"Christine, you don't have to do this," he pleaded with her.

Christine hit him in the back of the head with the butt of her gun to silence him. Ali couldn't help but shudder as her expression remained emotionless.

"She's doing what I want her do to," Gemma replied.

Ali and Caden whipped their heads around, trying to find her.

"Silly, Morgan's. I'm right in front of you."

The realization nearly sent Ali to her knees for a second time. Gemma's voice was coming through Christine.

"But… how?" Caden whispered.

Her answer was a high, cruel laugh. "Aww, does it matter, baby?" Gemma answered, returning to the childish sarcasm of before, making Caden bristle at the endearment. "Oh, what's the matter?" she continued to tease. "Don't like the way I look?" With that she made Christine do a twirl, laughing hysterically. "Ah ah ah," she scolded, when Zach tried to stand again. "You wouldn't want me to make her hit you again, would you?"

Zach glared at the ground, but remained quiet.

"How did you get Christine? She was--"

"What? Immune?" Gemma snapped, cutting Ali off. "No, she wasn't. I only made it seem like she was." A nasty smile curling her lips.

"Him too." She smirked, nudging the toe of Christine's shoe into Zach's knee.

"That's not true," Zach grunted, rubbing his knee when she withdrew her foot. "I've been fine since drinking that coffee. And I haven't had any water since!"

Gemma shook her finger at him as if she was reprimanding a small child. "That's what you thought about Christine too, remember?"

With that Gemma snapped her fingers, bringing Zach to his feet and taking the gun.

"See what I mean?" Gemma replied, now projecting

from Zach.

Ali and Caden couldn't believe their eyes.

Christine was holding her head, as if she was waking up from an all-nighter and had a bad headache. "What happened?" she asked, bringing her eyes to meet Ali's. "Why are we in an alley?" She turned to look at Zach and her eyes widened, the gun now pointing at her.

"Zach! What are you doing?" She gasped.

"Oh, he's just doing what I tell him to do," Gemma replied.

Christine's eyes grew as large as saucers as what was going on became clear. "Gemma? But--"

Gemma let out a sigh and placed one hand on Zach's hip, making the sight of Zach's six foot two inch frame comical.

"Please, not that again." She lowered the gun down once more, then with another snap of the fingers, she returned to Christine's body, quickly taking the gun away from a confused Zach. "You guys are *so* chatty!" She tucked Christine's hair behind her ear, sounding exasperated.

"What do you want, Gemma?" Ali demanded, infuriated that Gemma not only had found a way to infect her friends, but that she hadn't figured it out.

"What do I want?" she repeated, fake surprise in her voice. "Why, I want you and Caden, of course."

"But why! Why us? What did we do?" As hard as she tried not to, she couldn't help her voice cracking on those last words. *I will not give this bitch the satisfaction of seeing me cry.*

"It's not what you did; it's what you *didn't* do."

Ali could feel Caden moving closer to her, willing her to be quiet.

"What? You mean not becoming one of your mindless followers." The words tasted like acid coming out of her mouth.

"Ali, you amuse me." Gemma laughed, flicking something from Christine's nails. "It's true that you and Caden weren't affected by the… little *additive* I put in the water, and it's also true that we want to study you."

Suddenly without notice, Ali dove for Caden's jacket and pulled out the Smith & Wesson he had tucked away in there.

"Ali! What are you doing?" Caden asked, jumping back in surprise.

Ali's hands were shaking, but she held the gun up, pointed directly at Gemma.

"Let them go, Gemma!" Ali demanded. As Ali expected, Gemma began to laugh. "I mean it!" she yelled, although she made sure the words weren't as strong.

"Ali, Ali, Ali." She took a step forward, still remaining in Christine's body. "What are you going to do? Shoot me?"

She snapped her finger, "or me?"

Ali whipped the gun towards Zach, but by the time she had focused on his body, Gemma had returned to Christine's.

"Oh! I know," Gemma squealed with delight, "why don't you just shoot both of them! Then that will be two less people I'll need to dispose of."

Ali's gaze clouded, she knew that she wasn't going to shoot either one of her friends, but she needed to ensure that Gemma wouldn't search her. There wasn't any way out of this, she knew it and Gemma knew it too.

"Oh, is little Ali having trouble shooting her best friend?" She pushed the muzzle of the shotgun into Zach's back, nudging him to stand. "Move it, lover boy."

Zach walked forward, towards Ali, the gun digging into his lower back. "Take the gun," she instructed.

Ali looked into Zach's face and saw the hatred that burned deep within. She prayed that he would read the apology within her eyes before giving him a tiny shake of her head, letting him take the gun away from her.

"Now pass it back to me."

Zach passed the weapon back to her.

Pulling a piece of zip tie from her pocket, Gemma passed it to Caden.

"Now, tie your sister's hands together."

Resigned, Caden took the piece of plastic and tied Ali's hand behind her back. As the zip tie bit into Ali's wrist, she gave her brother a rueful glare, wondering why he had to tie them so tight.

Probably still trying to do the big brother thing and to keep her from doing something else rash and stupid, he was almost certainly angry at her for throwing him under the bus. She only wished that she had had time to explain why she had done it, hopefully, she still would.

"Your turn, baby." She handed Zach another zip tie and motioned for him to do the same to Caden.

As they turned to face Gemma again, a cruel smile played on her lips. "See? That wasn't so hard, was it?"

The sickingly sweet sound of her voice, made Ali's stomach churn.

"Now, we're going to go to the car and go for a little ride."

Gemma had Zach drive, the gun that Caden carried firm in her hand, the shotgun by her feet. Ali and Caden had managed to get into the backseat without falling over. Although, Ali was pleased that her hunch was correct. Gemma hadn't searched her.

The gun was still tucked into the small of her back. They sat in silence, stone-faced as they drove east; Ali couldn't imagine where she was taking them. Her mind raced with pictures of abandoned houses, run-down buildings and large empty spaces. Places where no one could hear their screams for help. Not that there was anyone to help anyway.

As they continued on, Ali realized that they were being taken towards Mount Lemmon, the place they were camping when the first quake happened. She held her breath as they drove on past the turning point, going further east than Ali had ever been.

The surroundings were different than what she was used to, they drove past farms and horse stables, large sprawling houses set in a country club. This was where Gemma told Zach to turn.

"I'm really not dressed for eighteen holes." Caden smirked, as they drove through the course. Gemma just threw him a cool look, before returning her attention to the road.

"Follow it all the way to the end," she instructed.

Weeping Willows draped themselves over algae covered ponds with spouting water fountains. This was a place that Ali would have loved to have visited if the circumstances had been different. A few minutes later, Zach pulled into the circular drive of a large adobe style home.

"Well, here we are!" Gemma happily announced, as if they were there to visit family and friends, and not as captives. She ordered everyone out of the car, the gun still on Zach, discouraging any type of plan Caden or Ali may have been devising.

"Alright, in you go," she said.

In single file, they walked into a gated courtyard, towards a heavy wood double door. It was ornately carved with symbols and words that Ali did not recognize.

"Beautiful, isn't it?" Gemma whispered into her ear, causing her to jump.

Gemma pushed the door open and motioned for them to go inside. The house was dimly lit, the shutters closed. Ali stumbled over the threshold, not noticing the small decline. Catching herself, she entered into a large foyer that opened into a family room with comfortable plush sofas, a very large television and gorgeous views of the Rincon Mountains.

"Well, go ahead and sit down," Gemma offered. The normalcy of her demeanor continued to throw them off.

"What are you going to do with us?" Caden asked sourly, plopping down into one of the armchairs as directed.

Gemma just smiled and finished tying Zach's hands

together, as he sat on the sofa across from him.

Ali remained standing, taking in their surroundings. It was a very nice house that didn't seem to have any damage, much like the Burke's home when they went to search for Gemma.

"Ali, be a dear and tighten this for me," Gemma requested, holding her hands together with a zip tie partially around them.

Giving her a quizzical look, Ali pulled the tie together and watched as Gemma tested the tightness.

"Well, now that you are all secure, I think I'm going to return to my own body," Gemma stated, wrinkling her nose as she looked down at Christine's. "Don't worry; you'll be seeing me again soon."

Suddenly Christine's body dropped to ground and everyone let out a cry of surprise. Zach hastily stood and moved to her, checking to see if she was still breathing. When he touched her, she began to stir.

"Oh thank, God." Ali whispered.

"Christine?" Zach's voice was full of hope and doubt. "Christine, is that you?"

Christine blinked her eyes twice, and then looked up at Zach. "Zach? Zach what happened? Where are we?" She tried to sit up but realized her hands were bound together by zip ties. "How did my hands get tied? What's going on?" Her breathing began to quicken, her body shaking. "Why don't I remember anything?"

Ali walked to her other side and kneeled next to Christine. "Shh," she soothed. "We've been captured by Gemma. We are at their... their... well to be honest; I have no idea where we are. Their headquarters, I guess," Ali offered weakly, not wanting to leave her uninformed, but also not wanting to give her the wrong information.

Christine looked around the large room. "It doesn't look like a headquarters, it looks like a house."

Caden snorted at the blunt correctness of her statement. Even Ali felt a small tug pulling at her mouth.

"So, your plans working?" Christine asked her, giving her a hard look.

"Well, I was able..." Ali cut herself off, looking over at Caden. She had just remembered that it was no longer safe to speak to Christine or Zach.

From the look Caden was sending her, he remembered

too.

"You were able to do what?" Christine asked.

Taking a deep breath, Ali answered, "I was able to get us in a real jam. Wasn't I?"

Christine's face softened and she scooted herself closer to Ali. "It's okay," she said, as she gave Ali a playful nudge on the shoulder. "We'll figure out something to get out of here."

Big fat tears fell down Ali's cheeks.

"Oh, babe, don't cry."

Christine wished her hands were free to give her a hug. Ali wished she could tell her that the tears had nothing to do with them being captured.

Caden stood and helped them to their feet. Christine and Zach sat together on the sofa while Caden returned to the armchair. Ali began pacing the room, trying to figure out what to do. With her hands tied in front of her, she couldn't reach the gun.

She couldn't ask Christine to do it since she wasn't

entirely positive that Gemma wouldn't read her thoughts. She could ask Caden... but she wasn't sure how to get him alone or where to hide the gun.

"Ali, will you please stop pacing, you're driving me crazy," Caden growled at her.

His mood was getting considerably darker by the minute. She stuck her tongue out at him, realizing that getting into an argument with him now would be useless and sat down on a bench next to the window.

The sun was setting, the sky streaking with oranges, pinks and blues. Looking around the room she tried to eye a light switch or a lamp.

"I wonder if she expects us to sit here in the dark," Ali mused, getting to her feet again, nervous energy coursing through her.

Walking around the room, she found a switch and flicked it on. Light flooded the area. She continued to walk back towards the foyer, then down a small hall that led to the kitchen. Fumbling with the drawers she wasn't surprised when she found them empty.

Leaning against the counter she relished in the silence, giving her time to think. She knew that they were going to have to tell Christine *and* Zach that they were infected, but she didn't know how and she was dreading their reactions.

She could only assume that Caden's bad mood had come from the same realization… and being tied up.

Walking back into the living room, everyone had gone still, tension in the air.

"What? What's happening?" she asked, entering the room and then coming to a halt.

Standing in front of her was Gemma. Ali was shocked. She had been standing in the kitchen, close to the front door and hadn't heard anyone come in. Gemma twisted around to face her.

"Ali!" she exclaimed, as if surprised to see her. She walked over to her and took her arms. "Come on, we can't have this discussion without you."

Ali's feet tripped over each other as she was dragged back into the room with the others. Gemma pushed her onto the sofa next to Christine before walking around the coffee table and stood in front of them, her face now set in a grim mask.

No one spoke, waiting for her to make the first move.

Clasping her hands behind her back, she began to pace in a small circle, shaking her head as she went.

"Get on it with Gemma," Caden spat out, his eyes full of contempt.

Gemma stopped, and tilted her head in his direction. "Oh, Caden," she whispered. She walked up to the chair and then sat on his lap. "I really was fond of you." She leaned her head in for a kiss, but Caden turned his face away.

To Ali's surprise, Gemma looked hurt, but quickly covered it up. Standing up again, she came to the sofa and stood in front of Zach. "It's time to dispose of you."

Gemma said it so smoothly, so calmly that Zach actually laughed.

"Get rid of me," he snorted. "Why get rid of me? I'm immune remember?" He looked over at Christine and Ali.

Christine's face was full of astonishment, Ali's dread.

"Zach," she began, but before she could finish, Gemma laid herself on the ground. Closing her eyes, her body went limp.

"What the hell?" Christine whispered.

A split second later, Christine rose, breaking the zip tie free. "I'm sorry, Zach," Gemma's voice spoke. "I really thought that they would have had the guts to tell you," she paused, as Christine's body walked over to Gemma's lifeless one and pulled Caden's gun from her jacket pocket.

"Tell me what?" Zach asked; sweat beginning to shine on his forehead.

"That you weren't immune and that you're going to die."

Without any further warning, she pulled the trigger.

Ali screamed as blood splattered onto her and the wall behind them. Zach turned his head and looked at her, his eyes wide with shock, before looking down at his hand holding his stomach and falling to the ground.

The gun was next to Gemma's body now and Christine was looking at her hands, bewildered on how she was suddenly free. When she looked up, her face was frozen in a silent scream.

Kneeling over him, Christine reached out to hold Zach's hand, but he jerked it back.

Stung, she flinched.

"Zach," she whispered, reaching her hand out again.

Using what little strength he had left, he clutched her hand, moving his lips but no words came out.

Moving closer to him, she kept whispering "I love you" over and over. He made another attempt to speak, blood beginning to stream out the corner of his mouth.

Everyone held their breath as he whispered, "I love you, too."

Then he was gone.

This death wasn't like DJ's; quick, painless.

Zach's voice choked off into a gurgle, as blood poured from his mouth. His eyes rolled into the back of his head and then he went limp.

Christine suddenly let out a cry. "What happened?" she demanded, clutching Zach's body to hers, blood seeping into her shorts and t-shirt. Out of the corner of her eye, she could see Gemma push herself up off the floor.

Christine held Zach closer as Gemma walked over to her and took the gun from where it had fallen, reaching for Christine's hands to restrain them again. Christine let out a low growl, making Gemma stop.

She just shrugged and whispered, "It doesn't matter any way."

With that, she got up and left them alone.

Ali's face was streaked with tears and Caden was as still as a statue. Christine looked to Ali for answers, but nothing came. How was she supposed to tell her best friend that she had killed the love of her life without realizing it?

"Someone say something!" Christine shrieked between gasps of air.

Ali moved closer to her, kneeling down and awkwardly lifting her arms to bring them down around Christine.

"It was Gemma," she whispered, Caden nodding her on. "She... she..." Tears where thick in her throat.

"She what?" Christine nearly shouted, her eyes had turned steely at the mention of Gemma's name.

"She... she took... she took over your body." She couldn't do it. Ali couldn't tell her.

"She used you to kill Zach," Caden finished quietly.

Christine's body went limp, her breathing still. Ali was

thankful that she had her arms wrapped around her, preventing her from falling completely to the ground.

While trying to keep Christine upright in this awkward position, Ali was able to experience the odd sensation of one body remaining warm while the small bit of Zach's body that she touched was cooling.

Is he supposed to cool that fast?

"Christine?" she whispered into her ear.

"Don't." Christine's voice was hard, void of all emotion. "Just don't."

Caden moved to kneel beside Zach.

"It wasn't your fault, Chris, she… it wasn't… you had no control."

CHAPTER THIRTEEN

Silence.

All Ali heard was silence. The sun had gone down; the family room was now awash in the soft glow of a lamp. They sat in a loose circle around Zach's body, feeling strange about hovering, however wanting to protect him from... them. The silence was beginning to become unbearable, but no one knew what to say.

Looking over to Christine, Ali thought *How do you comfort someone that feels they don't deserve it?*

Caden had been able to give her a blanket and wrap it around her shoulders at first, but she had let it drop almost immediately. After a few more attempts he just let it fall around her and returned to his seat, defeated. Their gazes would inadvertently cross path, quickly moving away if they were caught looking.

With a sigh, Ali stood to move over to Caden to be in his warmth. As she maneuvered around Zach, she was hit hard by a thought.

The realization that she hadn't put effort into trying to offer her best friend comfort made her stumble over her feet. Even though she had witnessed it first hand, that she knew it was Gemma that really killed Zach and that Christine would never have hurt them on purpose if she had control; she was afraid of her now. A cold chill ran down her spine, how could she be afraid of Christine? *Because of that bitch, Gemma, that's why.*

"You're not safe around me."

Ali gasped, afraid that she had spoken her fears out loud.

A sad smile tugged at Christine's lips. "Ali, we've been best friends for years, you really don't think I know what's going through your mind?" She turned herself towards them. "Think about it." She paused to struggle with the blanket. "She knew exactly where we were and what we were doing because of me and Zach. Anything we would attempt now would be absolutely pointless." She plopped down in between Caden and Ali, looking her dead in the eye. "You have to get rid of me." Her voice was flat, lifeless.

Final.

Tears welled into Ali's eyes. She thought of her mother and Zach, and of DJ. Her head began to shake violently.

"No." She couldn't do it, not again. "No. We find

another way." She looked to her brother for confirmation.

Caden remained quiet, his face a blank mask.

"Caden?" Ali whispered, needing him to be with her on this, despite her messed up way of planning in the past.

They had to find something, anything to make up for what she had led them into.

"Ali," Christine began, reading Caden's silence as agreement with her. "You guys can't do anything if I'm still with you. Face it; she can make me do anything at any time." Letting out a sigh, she fell back into the couch. "And don't say you'll just leave me behind, because if you do then I'll just be used to track you down." Tears began to fall freely. "And I wouldn't want to be a part of that."

"No, we will find a way to get you through this, to find a cure--"

Christine stood then, anger flashing in her eyes, cutting Ali off. "What does it matter anyway? I'm disposable! I'm not one of the keys," she sneered. "You guys are the 'key'," flinging the blanket away from her. "No matter what happens after this, I'm dead!"

Ali flinched at her last words.

"Don't you get it? I'm dead," Christine whispered.

Tears began to flow from both their eyes. Ali stood wishing her hands weren't bound and she could give Christine some sort of comfort, but Christine retreated to sit next to Zach again, deterring any further conversation. Ali took a step back, knocking into the couch and nearly falling on top of Caden.

"Will you please say something," Ali growled through gritted teeth.

What the hell is with him! She needed him to help her convince Christine that they could get out of this; that they would come up with a real plan this time. She reached her hands out and tried to move his face towards hers, but he refused to budge.

"Damn it, Caden Alexander Morgan, don't give up on me!" The words flew from her mouth before she had time to think them.

Caden looked at her with shock in his eyes. "Ali… I would nev--" but before he could say what he would never do, they heard the front door open and the click of heels on the tile.

Christine's body grew rigid but she remained seated

next to Zach, her eyes hard as stone, fixed upon the wall opposite them.

"Oh, don't stop your talking on my account," Gemma stated, as she breezed into the room wearing a blue maxi dress. She looked like she was going to a party. "I would love know what Caden was going to say next." Gemma gave him a saucy wink as Ali kept quiet, slumping next to Caden, irritated that she already knew everything they were talking about.

"What? No bodyguard?" Caden asked her, lifting his eyebrow.

Gemma settled herself into the recliner closest to them. "No, I realized that won't be necessary." Her gaze flickering to Zach and Christine. "With one less person now."

The silence that had momentarily disappeared returned with a cold, hard vengeance. Letting out an impatient sigh, Gemma returned to her feet.

"Well, if you guys want to be that way about it, I guess it's time to clean up here and move you to a more… permanent facility."

Ali could feel Caden straighten out of his slouch next to

her.

"What do you mean by 'permanent?'" he asked her, his voice cool, sounding bored even, visibly throwing Gemma off her game.

Trying to recover herself, she brought time by smoothing her dress. "Well, it won't be a secret for much longer anyway; we need to begin our tests on you and the others."

All their ears pricked up at the mention of other people.

"Others? Like us?" Ali asked, unable to keep the hope out of her voice.

"Not exactly." Gemma smiled. "Let's just say that the additive had unexpected results." She walked over to Christine and placed a hand on her shoulder, at first Ali was shocked that Christine hadn't shaken her off, but then realized Gemma must be controlling her again.

Like a master puppeteer, Gemma silently commanded Christine to rise, lifting Zach in the same movement. Ali and Caden both let out a gasp, Christine had always been a strong person, but she had never been able to lift Zach like this.

Giving each other a quick look, they realized that Gemma was demonstrating just what she could have her do. At any time.

"Good, Christine, let's take him out back," Gemma instructed softly. Looking over her shoulder, "Now, you two stay put," she teased.

Ali and Caden watched through the large window as Christine walked to the nearest tree and gently laid Zach beneath it. Gemma followed behind with a white cloth they had not noticed her carrying before. To further their shock, Gemma kneeled next to his body and tucked the cloth around him like a blanket.

If anyone were to walk by, it would like as if Zach was simply sleeping instead of being dead.

A few moments passed before Christine leaned down and kissed Zach's head, taking the gun away from Gemma's hand. Together they walked back into the room. Ali looked closely at Christine's face, trying to see any recognition of her friend now. There was none.

With the gun now focused on Ali, Gemma gestured to the front door. Without another word, she and Caden rose to their feet and walked out in single file.

Caden and Ali sat in the back of a white minivan with the child locks engaged, while Christine drove them through the city. *Way to go, Ali. What a damn mess this is.* She scolded herself.

"Stop thinking like that," Caden whispered to her.

"What?" She turned to him; she knew that she hadn't said that out loud.

"It's not your fault, so shut up, your inner dialog is giving me a headache now," he whispered again.

She was about to ask him another question, but a quick jerk of his head made her remember that they were not alone.

Ugh, what in the hell is going on! Caden just began to chuckle.

"What is so funny back there?" Gemma demanded.

"Oh, nothing much, Mom," Caden answered, "just admiring the scenery."

Gemma looked out the window and saw nothing but darkness. "Funny, Caden."

Ali could hear Gemma roll her eyes for falling for that

one and bit the inside of her cheek to keep from laughing. Driving through the dark, deserted streets felt oddly comforting to Ali. The darkness allowing her the privacy she needed to freak out as she was doing now without an audience.

What Gemma had said about there being others had left her confused, did she mean other people like her and Caden? Others like Christine and Zach? How did the additive not work?

Or others that were there to study them?

A shiver ran down her spine at the thought of being used as a test subject. Caden jerked his head up looking over at her panic in his eyes. Ali gave him a questioning look; he stared intently into her eyes for a few seconds then turned away, perplexed.

Ali wanted to ask him what was going on, but had the feeling that it wasn't the time or the place.

Glancing out the windows Ali recognized that they were quickly approaching Grant Road. *How fast is Christine driving?* It took them at least an hour to get out to the house earlier, it had only been what? Twenty minutes tops?

"Pull over here, Christine." Gemma pointed to a gas

station, the lights glowed in welcome, but like the rest of the town, it appeared totally abandoned.

Without a word, Christine followed her orders.

Gemma opened the passenger door and then walked to the back of the van. Ali and Caden craned their necks trying to see what she was doing. In the darkness, they could only make out her shape rummaging around the back. When she returned, the light gleamed off two syringes that she was holding in her hand.

"Now, we can do this the easy way… which you guys really haven't been too keen on. Or, we can do this the hard way." She snapped her fingers and Christine trained Gemma's gun on Ali's head.

Resigning to their fate, Ali just nodded, holding her arms up in front of her.

"Good girl." Gemma smiled.

The needle stung like hell, a cool rush filling her veins, as the unknown liquid was pushed into them. She glared at Gemma as she threw that syringe over her shoulder, closing the door.

Before Gemma had gotten to Caden's side, Ali could

barely keep her eyes open. She could hear the van door slide open on Caden's side and a sharp intake of breath as the needle went into his arm. *Caden doesn't like needles, he needs to be…* What did Caden need to be?

Distracted, Ali, I need to be distracted. Yes! That was it. He needed to be distracted.

Why did that sound like Caden's voice?

❧

Ali woke up to a raging headache.

Ow, my head. She reached up and gingerly rubbed her temples.

"My hands are free!" she exclaimed, before instantly regretting it. Opening her eyes she found herself lying in a hospital room, with Caden in the bed across the room from her.

"Caden," she whispered.

He let out a moan before rolling over onto his side.

Sitting up, she placed one foot on the floor, steadying herself against the bed. *What in the hell did she give us?* She slowly walked over to Caden's bed and gently shook him.

"Caden," she said louder, realizing that her mouth and throat were dry.

"What?" he mumbled, still lying on his side.

"Caden, wake up." She gave him a shove into his back.

Uttering something that didn't quite sound like 'duck' he rolled over and grabbed his head.

"Did they drug us?" he asked as he sat up, squinting his eyes shut from the sunlight seeping into the room.

"Yeah, it must have been whatever she injected into us." Ali stretched her hands to rub her back and discovered her gun was gone.

"They took the gun!" she cried out.

"Ssshhh," Caden growled, clasping his hands over his ears, "are you really surprised? They've had plenty of time to search us." He glanced around for a clock. "How long have we been out anyway?"

With a shrug Ali retreated back to her bed, covering her face with the pillow. She knew they would search her eventually, but for some reason she thought she had more time.

Stop thinking, Ali. Just stop thinking, period.

"That is an excellent idea. If I can't take your yelling right now, I sure as hell can't take your crazy thought process either."

She sat up like a shot. "What?"

Caden let out a sigh and got out of bed.

Walking to the door, he half-heartedly tested it, knowing that it was locked. Next he looked out the window and discovered a guard was standing next to the door. Walking back over to Ali, he sat down on her bed and leaned in close to her, not sure if the room was wired or not.

"I can hear your thoughts." He grabbed her arm before she could ask any more questions. "I don't know how." He smiled when she gasped. "It just started yesterday, after… well, after Gemma killed Zach."

Ali gave him a doubtful look.

"You don't believe me? Fine, think about something."

My brother has lost his mind, what am I going to do now?

Caden nearly fell out the bed laughing. "You don't have

to worry about it; I'm still sane enough to help you."

Ali's eyes grew large. "Wait, is that why you were so quiet yesterday?"

He nodded his head.

"And what about that stuff with Gemma in the van?"

Again he shrugged.

"I was trying to see if she could read my thoughts… and I guess to see if I could get into her head." A type of sadness touched his voice that she didn't want to dig into.

"Can you teach me how to do it? I mean, do you even think I can?"

Caden looked at his sister and in that moment of eagerness; couldn't believe how much she looked like their mother.

"I think you can, I mean, out of everything else we've been though, why not?"

They both turned towards the door when the lock unlatched. Two people walked in; one pushing two food trays and the other holding what looked like aspirin.

Caden positioned himself in front of Ali, as she tried to

look around him.

"Take these; it will help your headaches," the young woman instructed them.

Caden eyed the pills warily.

"Why should we trust you?" Ali challenged.

The woman just rolled her eyes and set the pills down next to the food. "You're going to want to eat that too, the Midazolam she gave you guys will make you feel pretty yucky if you stay on an empty stomach."

They continued to sit on the bed as they watched them walk back out of the room.

"But it's up to you," she said with a shrug, motioning for the guard to relock the door.

"Do you think it's safe?" Ali asked, lifting the lid to reveal scrambled eggs, bacon, toast and a plastic cup of juice.

"Well, Gemma's been keeping us alive this long, why stop now?" He lifted his own lid and took a bite of the toast. "Taste's okay…" He then eyed longingly at the pills.

"Here, I'll try this one." She reached for two, popping

them into her mouth while ripping the foil off the juice cup. After a few minutes, Ali was still breathing.

They ate the rest of their breakfast while examining their room.

"Where do you think we are?" Caden asked her, looking out the window but only seeing a small courtyard surrounded by buildings.

"I have no idea. What was the last thing you remember?" Ali mumbled, as she ate her last piece of toast, her own memories clouded by the drugs they gave her.

"We were in a van with Gemma and Christine on our way back into town."

She nodded, encouraging him to go on.

"We had just hit Grant Road and Wilmont when Gemma told Christine to pull over." He shook his head as the last thoughts remained hidden. "That's all I got."

Ali let out a huff as that was all she remembered too.

"Well, that would have put us close to either Tucson Medical or St. Joe's Hospital." Since she had been to neither one, that wasn't much to go on.

QUAKE

"It has to be one of those," Caden agreed, since his hospital knowledge was as lacking as hers. "But why a hospital?" he mused, opening a door to reveal a private bathroom.

"Well, they want to study us, right? What better place." Ali's voice had become quiet and tears threatened to spill over. She was beyond exhausted, her head hurt, but most importantly she wanted to know where Christine was and if she was alright.

"Ali, stop, you're just going to drive yourself crazy thinking about it."

"Ugh! What's going to make me go crazy is you in my head all the time now!" She spat at him, immediately regretting her outburst. Reaching out her hand, "Just teach me how to do it, alright?"

Now it was Caden's turn to let out a huff. "Okay, I'll try, but I'm still not sure how *I* did it." He sat on her bed again and closed his eyes trying to remember. "First thing I did was go numb, ya know? After Zach." His voice dropped an octave, but he continued on. "After he died, I just felt empty. I didn't care what happened to us, that was when I first heard your thoughts, when I wasn't able to think at all."

Ali sat, staring at her brother with her mouth open. Zach had been Caden's best friend since they were in elementary school so Caden's lack of reaction had confused her and made her angry. She had no idea it went this deep. Pulling him into a hug, she vowed, then and there, not to do any more stupid stunts that may get herself, or him, killed.

Chuckling himself out of his funk, he added, "We'll see about that. Now the other part is… I can't turn it off. I can now hear you all the time." He emphasized the last words to make her fully understand. "I haven't been able to figure a way out yet. So once you hear me, you'll be stuck with my thoughts. Sure you're ready?"

Ali nodded at him solemnly.

"Ok, relax your mind," Caden instructed. "That's how I heard your thoughts about Chris at the house."

A light blush lit Ali's cheeks.

"Don't worry about it, sis, I thought the same thing." He gave her an encouraging squeeze, "Now, relax."

Ali gave a snort, but lay down on the bed and took a deep breath.

This is ridiculous, she thought.

"Ali," Caden's voice was full of exasperation.

Mentally sticking her tongue out at him, she took another deep breath, closing her eyes as she tried to empty her mind. It wasn't easy. Thoughts of her mother, DJ and Zach rapidly flashed through her mind.

"Damn it, Ali, stop! I don't want to re-live that shit!"

"Well, excuse me, Mr. I Was Numb When I Did It!" She knew she was being unfair, knew that she was yelling, knew that there was someone outside their door, but she no longer cared.

"I don't know how to quiet my mind after everything that we've been through! I want to be numb more than anything, but I just can't."

"I know you've said that it isn't my fault, that I had no way of knowing that we would end up here no matter what we did, but I can't help feeling that if we had brought Mom with us, or if DJ hadn't had fallen in love with me... if I had made an actual plan before we went to the Armory, maybe, just maybe they all would be alive."

There she had said it. She had finally said out loud

everything that had been eating her up inside.

Caden stood rooted to the ground. He knew that Ali felt guilty from her thoughts, but she had never put them together like that.

"So, while you say 'relax your mind,' it isn't that damn easy!" She stormed off to the bathroom and let the door slam behind her.

To her surprise she found that it had been stocked with toothbrushes, towels and clothing. Granted, they were hospital scrubs but they were clean and looking down at her blood crusted clothing she desperately wanted to change. Glancing over to the shower she noticed a note was tacked to the showerhead.

The water is safe.

"Well, hell's bells," she snorted out. Turning the water on she saw that is was clear again and placed her hand under the warm stream to see if she would have a reaction to it. The sparks were there but not as bright so the water must still contain some of the additive that Gemma had placed into it.

Stripping down she stepped into the warm stream of water and let it run over her. The tension in her back lessened, and her head felt lighter as the water ran through her braids.

She rubbed at the dried blood on her skin and watched as the water turned a russet color as it washed away. Biting her lower lip to stop the tears she reached for the shampoo bottle; and it happened.

She heard him.

His thoughts were agitated, but she heard him, her mind had opened up.

Quickly finishing her shower, she dressed in the scrubs and exited the bathroom with a shy smile on her face.

"What are you so happy about?" Caden asked, pacing the room.

"I love you too."

He stopped pacing and looked at her.

"I know, I'm a handful and that I should know better, Caden," she continued to repeat his thoughts back to him. "And I will always trust you." She was swept off her feet into a bear hug and felt moisture on her cheek.

When Caden set her down, there were tears falling

from in his eyes.

"You did it!" He beamed like the proud brother he was. "You finally did it, but how?"

Ali just shrugged as she still wasn't sure about it. She told him about the scrubs and the toiletries in the bathroom and shooed him in there to give her some space for a few moments.

Knowing that Caden would hear what she was thinking, she willed herself to keep her mind clear, just to sit in the silence and let it be for a minute.

It was soothing, sitting on the hospital bed in silence. The only other time she had been to a hospital was when her grandfather had died. The sound of the machines beeping, the oxygen machine's wheezing and all the wires and IV's had made her extremely upset. She had only remained in the room because her mother had had a death grip on her hand and wouldn't let go. Being here now; with just two beds set up and a bodyguard at the door, it was almost reassuring.

Closing her eyes and leaning back on the pillow, she allowed her thoughts to flow freely again, hearing Caden let out a laugh when she thought about how nice it would be if they could just stay here in this room if they weren't being held hostage by a psychotic bitch.

Without meaning to, she thought about Christine, wondering what Gemma had done with her.

Caden stepped out of the bathroom and shook his head, meaning that he didn't know either.

CHAPTER FOURTEEN

The beeping of the heart rate monitor began to annoy Ali. She was lying on a table, with electrodes attached to her pulse points. She had been counting the ceiling tiles until Caden silently told her to stop. She scowled him in her mind and heard him chuckle, they were still working on shutting the other out of their thoughts, but so far, no luck.

They had been at the hospital for five days now. Every morning after breakfast they were brought into the same examination room. Ali had lost count of how many vials of blood had been taken from her, the latest batch leaving her woozy.

Lifting her arm slightly, she saw that the bruising and track marks were getting worse and briefly wondered what people would think when they saw her, only to remember that she was being held against her will and the only people that would see her were medical staff.

One of which passed by, carrying a silver tray full of instruments to the room next door.

She knew that it was the operating room. She heard the muted voices of the doctors and nurses' discussing whoever or whatever was being operated on. Caden had been thinking about who it could possibly be and if there were others like them.

It doesn't make sense for there to be others like us, since Gemma keeps saying we are the 'key,' Ali argued.

Yeah, but she also said there were others that didn't change, he argued back, *others where something went wrong.*

Ali rolled her eyes, and then quickly looked around to make sure no one had noticed. *Yes, dear brother, but she also said that she killed everyone that didn't change. So I'm pretty sure we can't count on her as a reliable source of information.*

Caden let out a loud sigh.

"Anything wrong?" the nurse asked him, immediately checking the monitor and cables.

"Yeah, being here."

The nurse gave him a cross look, but went back to the little desk in the corner.

Will you please be careful? Ali scolded.

So far, their new talent hadn't been discovered and they both knew what would happen if it was: the operating room. He thought of a few choice words, but didn't bring any more attention to himself. Ali decided to focus on the nurse and various staff they have seen.

They appeared to be human; some had that strange dazed look about them that told her they were more than likely under the effects of Gemma, but most acted perfectly fine. They would only ask the minimal questions and when Ali or Caden tried to speak with them, they would never answer back.

Once all the testing was done for the day, they were returned to their rooms and left alone. Ali tried to look into the other rooms to see if she could catch a glimpse of Christine, but there was no sign of her.

Ali feared for the worst, but Caden told her to keep holding out hope.

"Why should I?" Ali had pouted on the third day, watching rain fall from the window.

She had been sore, cranky and bored. The TV didn't work and talking with Caden about trivial things had been exhausting.

"Maybe they need her," he replied, lying on the bed with his arm over his eyes. She hadn't even bothered to reply.

Now she wondered if it was true. Did they need her? And if so, why? And another question that had been nagging at her… where was Gemma?

Ali got her answer the next day.

"Rise and shine, Morgan's." The orderly from their first day came in, holding two hospital gowns.

Shit, Caden thought.

"What are those for?" Ali asked, afraid that she already knew the answer.

"Examination day," the orderly answered briskly.

They exchanged glances with each other.

"What do you mean? Haven't we already been examined?"

The orderly remained quiet, gesturing with her hand towards the bathroom.

"Can't you please just tell us?" Ali nearly begged, a vision of the surgical instruments she had seen earlier flashing through her mind.

Again, the orderly just pointed to the bathroom. Caden let out a frustrated sigh, but got up and went to change.

Keep trying.

"Well, since you bring us food every day, can you at least tell me your name?"

The orderly turned towards her and crinkled up her face, debating on what she should say. "Thompson," she replied. "You can call me Thompson."

"Okay, Thompson, what are they going to do to us?"

Thompson shook her head. "I can't tell you that."

Groaning, Ali tried again. "Where are we?" She could see this gave Thompson another pause. Ali then added, "Please?" She inserted just a touch of sadness into her voice.

Thompson gave out a sigh, but before she could answer there was another knock on the door.

"They want them now," another orderly announced before shutting the door.

Whatever connection Ali and she had been building was suddenly gone.

"Get changed, and then knock on the door when you're done." Thompson turned and nearly ran out of the room.

"Interesting," Caden said, as he walked out of the bathroom dressed in the gown. "She might be able to help us, if we can get her to stay long enough."

Ali let out a huff of air and walked into the bathroom only to quickly return dressed in the gown.

Are you seriously worried about your legs right now? Caden sent out.

"Get out of my head," Ali muttered before sticking her tongue at him and knocking on the door.

The orderly that had interrupted the conversation herded them down the corridor. As they made the last turn to their normal exam room Ali felt herself break out into a sweat.

What are they going to do, C? She felt him reach out his hand to her.

I don't know.

Grasping hands, they walked through the exam room to the operating room. At the sight of the gleaming silver

249

instruments, Caden stood defensively in front of Ali.

The orderly let out a snort before locking the door behind him. The room was bright and cold, with no windows to allow them to see the outside.

"Caden, I'm scared," Ali whispered, tightening her grip on his hand.

He wanted to tell her that he was too, but knew that would only undo her further.

"It's going to be okay, Ali, we'll be okay." His voice came out clear and strong, but she thought she detected a slight waver at the end. "We will," he said one more time.

The operating room door opened and three people wearing pale blue scrubs and masks over their faces looked up. As usual, the staff said nothing to them as they prepped the two separate areas for them.

After what felt like an eternity, but was probably likely five minutes, one of the masked staff turned to them and said, "We need the girl on the first table, you on the second." It was a woman's voice.

Caden felt Ali begin to shake behind him. He pushed her back against the wall and shook his head 'no.'

"No, we aren't getting on those tables unless you tell us what is going on," he demanded.

The first masked person looked over their shoulder and nodded their head. The other two figures began to walk towards them.

"We don't want to hurt you," the second figure, a man, held up a syringe filled with a milky white substance. "But we will if we have to."

Tears were streaming down Ali's face.

"What are you going to do to us?" Caden was frantically looking around the room for something to use as a weapon, to keep them safe.

"Last chance."

The masked figures were surrounding them and he thought he saw one push a small button on the counter, an alarm probably.

Ali buried her head in his back; *We don't have a choice.* He knew she was right, but his instinct to protect her was stronger than his will to give in.

C, let me go. Ali straightened her shoulders and began to walk around him. Caden threw his arm out to stop her, but she ducked it. Without a word, she walked to the first table and lay down, shutting her eyes.

He could see underneath her bravado that she was shaking lightly. The figures turned to him and he followed suit, lying on the bed designated for him.

Unlike Ali, he kept his eyes open. He followed the masks around the room with his eyes as they prepped the instruments they would be using; syringes, scalpels, something that reminded him of the tongs his mother used to use to pull spaghetti noodles out of the boiling water after he or Ali used the strainer to play in the dirt.

Once they had put everything in place, they began to pull a curtain between them.

"Please don't?" Caden begged.

For some odd reason he felt that if that curtain closed he would never see his sister again. The mask silently consulted his partner and with a shrug and a nod the curtain remained open.

The final mask walked over to Caden's table as they strapped him down.

"I think you're going to wish that you had them close

that curtain."

Caden's blood began to run cold.

It was Gemma.

"What are you doing here?" he asked her.

"This is just a little hobby of mine," she replied.

Caden could picture the smile she had on her face behind that mask. "Don't you dare hurt her--"

"Or what?" she cut him off. "You're not going to get out of this one." She spat out, anger replacing her overly sweet demeanor.

"You and your sister have resisted the mind control organism that was placed in the water supply," she continued, as she walked over to strap down Ali. "We even tried giving you a straight dose of the organism while you were knocked out and still... nothing."

Ali's eyes where hard and a cold, steely grey as Gemma looked down on her.

"We thought it was a defect and tried it out on the few others that seemed resistant but," she trailed off walking back to the center of the room, "turns out, they weren't.

And having the organism inserted in that high a dose had… dire results."

To Ali, Gemma tried to sound sad, but the gleam in her eye belied the truth.

"So, now, we are going to see what makes you two just so damn special."

She picked up a scalpel and held it in her hand, tapping it lightly against her index finger.

"Who wants to go first?"

Ali and Caden remained quiet.

"Ahh, so I get to use the scientific method, do I?" she mused.

"Alright then. Eeny, meany, miney, moe." She let out a girlish giggle that sent chills down both their spines.

"Caden," she stated her voice hard.

She walked over to him and placed the scalpel directly over his heart.

"Let's start with you, shall we?"

Ali was balled up on her side, tears freely flowing. They had been wheeled back into their room and deserted.

Yes, deserted, seems to fit, Caden agreed with her.

He felt that the only way they had survived Gemma's torture was by their still secret gift. Gemma had taken an almost perverse joy in the tests that had been done.

Looking over to his sister, he knew that she wasn't going to be able to close her eyes without seeing the scalpel slice into her skin as tissue samples where painfully taken.

They had both showered and dressed in clean scrubs.

Gingerly, he sat up and moved to his sister. She slowly scooted over and made room for him on her bed. Gently gathering her up in his arms, he began to hum the lullaby that their mother had made up for them when they were young. After the second verse, he heard Ali singing along in her mind, a vision of their mother shining bright.

Now I lay you down to sleep, I pray your closed eyes will keep.

Mama's tired it's been a long day, and it's time to sleep no longer to play.

I love you so please don't get me wrong, but Mom kind of sucks making up songs.

Ali and Caden always got a giggle out of hearing their mom trying to make up songs, especially this one when they both had a horrendous cold and were tired and cranky little monsters. It was always their favorite, it being the stupidest song she ever made up.

Get down!

Caden jerked his head up. "What?"

Ali turned her head to look up at him. "Why, what?" she asked.

"You just thought to get down."

Ali looked at him curiously. "No, I didn't. I was just listening to you hum."

Caden began to worry that maybe she wasn't handling the testing as well as she seemed to be.

Grab her and get down, now, damnit!

The urgency in the voice made Caden move. As soon as he had grabbed Ali and brought her down to the ground all hell broke loose.

The sound of gun fire erupted in the halls around them. Ali screamed, but stayed down on the ground close to Caden.

Stay down; we're coming to get you.

"Who is that?" Ali yelled over the noise. Caden just shook his head and remained crouched over her. There was suddenly a shrill whistle then the loudest boom they had ever heard.

The glass in the door shattered and the roof shook, sending pieces of the ceiling down around them like rain. Ali's eyes grew wide.

"Was that a missile?!"

Before Caden could think of a response the door flew open revealing a large man wearing a sleeveless black shirt with gray camouflage pants holding an assault rifle.

"Caden, Ali let's go!" he called to them.

They both remained frozen on the spot.

"Let's go!" he yelled again.

Caden stood and pulled Ali with him.

"Who are you?" he demanded.

Can we trust him? Ali asked.

Caden shrugged in response.

Look we don't have time for this, come on. NOW!

With one last glance at Ali, Caden grabbed her hand and made for the door.

The chaos they met when they got out of their room astonished them.

The hospital floor was a war zone. Several people Ali had never seen before were converging on the hospital staff, most of which were now armed with weapons.

A soft green light fell upon her and the man pulled her out of the way seconds before the wall behind her exploded.

He shoved her towards the staircase. "Run!" he yelled.

She took off like a shot, with Caden right beside her. She saw the green light again and pulled him down before it could hit either one of them. At the staircase they were met by a woman wearing the same gear as the man who had saved them.

It was Thompson!

"This way!" she instructed, while handing them each a gun.

"Hope you know how to use those," she breathed out, guiding them down the stairwell.

"You have no idea," Caden replied smugly.

If they weren't trying to get away from this place, Ali might have laughed, but now she just removed the safety and cocked the gun.

The walls around them shook as another blast went off, debris falling all around them.

"Where are we going?" Ali called out, wondering why these people were helping them escape.

"A safe place," was all the answer she received.

Can we trust them? Ali asked Caden.

Do we have a choice?

A resounding *no* answered both of them.

They had reached the first floor and Ali could see the exit. Without speaking they all broke into a sprint, eager to reach the outside.

"Down!" Thompson shouted before reaching around her back and pulling her shotgun free.

Ali and Caden ducked, seconds before glass exploded around them.

"Let's go!" she urged, taking slow steps towards the opening and switching her shotgun for a .45.

Ali and Caden quickly fell in line, guns ready. When they stepped outside, Ali let out a gasp. Just beyond the parking lot was a thick patch of grass, mostly brown and dead. A dense forest of trees stripped of their leaves mixed with evergreens. The sky was filled with low steely gray clouds and the air was cold, making Ali's nose tingle and goose bumps rise on her exposed skin.

"Where the hell are we?" Caden asked.

They continued to run towards a black double cab truck, the engine idling.

"Get in the back," Thompson ordered, as she slid behind the wheel.

Looking out of the window, Ali gasped and grabbed Caden's arm. The man that had broken them out was running full tilt towards them with a body thrown over his shoulder.

She didn't want to hope, but could it be?

Be calm, Caden warned but Ali could hear the anxiety in Caden's thoughts, the hope that it was her, but scared about having her with them.

The man threw open the backdoor and gently handed an unconscious Christine to Caden.

"What happened to her?" Ali demanded only to; again, have her answer met with silence.

The man slid into the passenger seat and gave Thompson a nod. Hitting the gas, the tires squealed as she jumped the curb and headed away from the hospital. Ali was nearly distraught. The adrenaline of the escape was wearing off quickly and the sight of Christine cradled in Caden's lap, not waking up no matter how hard they tried frightened her.

What did they do to her? Ali was close to tears.

We didn't do anything.

Caden and Ali froze, realizing that they had heard his voice in their thoughts during the escape.

"Will someone, anyone, please tell us who you are and what is going on?" Caden asked, pinching the bridge of his nose.

Thompson exchanged a glance with the man and let out a long sigh.

"My partner here is Mason... Liam Mason. Your friend there was put into a medically induced coma by one of our inside men two days ago. This," she continued on, knowing she was about to be interrupted, "was necessary to ensure that one; no red flags were brought up. We just told Gemma that it was necessary due to the trauma that she has gone through."

She paused as the truck took a sharp turn.

"Secondly, and most importantly, to make sure that she wouldn't be able to tell anyone where we are going."

"But she'll be able to wake up, right?" Ali asked, brushing hair out of Christine's face.

"Yes, we'll wake her up once we get the cure secured. Until then, its nap time for Christine."

Ali's head was spinning. 'Inside' people had put Christine in a coma so they could take her with them during the escape. Who would want to rescue them?

Caden, what in the hell is going on?

"Where are we going?" Caden repeated, feeling as if they had been sucked into some alternative reality.

"Cleveland."

"WHERE?!" They shouted in unison.

"We are heading to Cleveland, Ohio. We were sent to retrieve you by our leader," Mason informed them.

"Who in the hell is your leader and why in the hell do they care about us?"

Mason shot Thompson one last glance before answering. "Our leader cares because… he's your father."

ACKNOWLEDGEMENTS

I don't even know where to start…

First and foremost THANK YOU to Christine and Shalisa for not laughing hysterically at me when I first told you about my dream, encouraging me through those first rough drafts, letting me bounce every insane idea I ever had about this book off you, for telling me when I was totally off base and for loving these characters along with me.

Christine, thank you for letting me use your name and the names of your loved ones.

Larry, I could not have giving Caden life without you. Thank you for your wonderful brotherly protectiveness and crazy one-liners that I was able to sprinkle throughout this story.

My Snarkies. Girls, thank you for letting me vent and moan and type out my frustrations and joys throughout this process, you all ROCK and I will never let you forget that.

To my family and friends, what else can I say?? Most of y'all have loved me from the beginning and supporting me in this process means more to me than words will ever be able to express.

Finally, thank you to my weapons specialist for answering all of my questions and encouraging me to do my research and figure out just what Ali would use and how she would use it. Never thought I would get into that part of the book... and the crossbow? That was for you! Thank you for truly caring and cheering me on in the background.

~Love,

Lisa

ABOUT THE AUTHOR

Lisa lives in Southern Arizona with her two sons. When not writing, she can be found curled up on her favorite chair with Kindle in hand, chauffeuring one (or both) of the boys to basketball practices/games or playing some mind-numbing game on her phone. She loves the color blue and can't get enough of Butter Pecan ice cream!

Find Lisa Online!

http://www.lisaawrites.com

www.facebook.com/lisaawrites

www.twitter.com/lisaawrites

Quake is Lisa's debut novel, AfterShock the exciting sequel is expected in the spring of 2014.